STARSEEKER

Flower of Tamaroon

DIANE GRONAS

Witt's End Press
Printed in United States of America
by Create Space, Charleston, South Carolina

Library of Congress Cataloguing-in-Publication Data on file.
Paperback ISBN 978-0-9910073-4-9

Dedicated to the spirit of creative invention,
and hope for a better future.

CONTENTS

1

STARSEEKER TEST
TREYA 9006

As Tamaroon, did Treya spin,
in a mist of swirling white clouds.
Its glistening snow, plunged all life,
toward a dark and pending doom.

THE SPACE SHUTTLE TURNED INTO LAUNCH position and the thruster gauges rose. Annie sat at the controls in a helmet and flight-suit. Rhythmically, her fingers danced over the flashing touch-panel spread before her, causing the huge hanger door to open. Tapping in the last sequence, her hand came to rest on the smooth steering pad. Today she would either pass the Starseeker test at Gosar castle to join missions in space, or give up the search for her parents on the lost planet of Tamaroon forever.

"Prepare to launch," she alerted the ship. Flight systems lit up the holoscreen in response to her command.

"Aye, Captain!" Chip, the young copilot buckled on his flight harness and sat rigid in his seat.

"Launch!" Annie commanded.

Chip pressed the red thruster button, and their ship shot through the launch bay doors into space. A multitude of stars in the heaven greeted them. Clusters of wispy clouds slowly swirled around planet Treya far below. Ice spreading over the planet threatened starvation and had left only a belt of green around the equator.

Chip flipped through news reports on a clear holoscreen floating before him. The Starseeker mission to locate new sources of food and heat on extremely rare planets was in the headlines. He stopped on a page labeled Starseeker Candidates and scrolled through the text. "The data stream indicates there are no other candidates piloting a star class shuttle at age twelve. This increases your odds of success by 8.3 percent."

"Don't tell me the odds." Annie frowned. "I'll just do my best on the test, and we'll see what happens." She quickly tapped the control panel. The flight screen displayed objects of various sizes approaching. "Entering Gambler's Alley," she announced.

"Oh no! Not the asteroid belt." Chip stiffly pressed himself back in his seat and was now at full alert.

Quiet music from side speakers grew louder with

a rapid electronic beat trumpeting as rugged rocks began rocketing by outside. The controls at Annie's touch, rolled and spun the ship around the flying projectiles.

Chip's hands clung to his seat. "Calculating the safest route," he reported. A holographic tracking screen appeared showing safe flight paths with curving colored lines.

Annie dove around a small asteroid and suddenly pulled up over a large group of floating rocks that threatened to crush the ship.

Chip cringed, grabbed his flight harness and closed his eyes.

Annie laughed when she saw his expression. "Don't fry your circuits, Chip. I have everything under control." Annie remained calm as she threaded the speeding ship along a safe course through the barrage of shooting debris in the shifting maze. One patch of asteroids after another flew by until Annie's flight pattern settled into a rhythmic flow.

Chip seemed relaxed with his eyes now open.

A dark shadow began to loom ahead. A huge asteroid approached and quickly grew in size.

"Oh no, I can't watch." Chip put his arms over his face. "We're going to crash and burn."

"Seriously—I never would have pegged you for such a wimp. Just watch, we'll be fine."

Chip reluctantly opened space between his arms to look. "You really should be more careful, Miss

Annie."

The dark shadow before them grew. There would soon be no escape.

"Oh, I really can't watch!" Chip whimpered and closed his eyes.

The tracking screen glowed with colored lines suggesting pathways around the asteroid. One by one they blinked out and dwindled to only one. It led to a dark fissure that cut the surface on the left side of the enormous rock. Its crushing form was upon them.

Pulling back on the left thruster, Annie banked the ship hard left and swooped in toward the dark hole. The deep crevasse opened into a cavernous tunnel. Diving into the darkness, the ship twisted into the cavern. Light from the ship skimmed over rocky ridges. The walls closed in and became closer as they flew deeper into the curving tunnel. Turns became tighter. Annie slowed the ship just enough to make the curves. Suddenly a wall in the gloom ahead appeared to cut off the end of the tunnel.

"Prepare for impact!" Chip cried before the ship passed the last ridge.

Annie quickly pulled down on the right thruster and the ship rolled around the last ridge where an opening was revealed that led back to open space. She shook her head with amusement at the shock and relief on Chip's face. "Maybe we should try something that has a slower pace."

Chip nodded as Annie tapped the controls. The

throbbing music slowed to a light rhythmic beat. Annie rolled the ship over and headed toward the misty horizon of Treya.

It seemed no time at all passed when the ship announced, "Re-entry complete." The forward shield opened and revealed the mountains and green valleys of Treya.

"Let's visit one of my favorite places," Annie said, as she keyed in a course for the Gosar Valley. Moments later, the ship was slip sliding along a curving groove in a valley of trees. The small ship lifted up and grazed over the tips of tall pines. They plunged toward a small creek bed on the other side and quickly pulled up into a double barrel spin.

Chip shut his eyes. "If I don't watch, it won't affect me."

"Fine!" Annie had not been surprised by Chip's reaction and was callously amused by his discomfort. "Our time is almost up anyway. I have to meet Uncle Jordan soon. Let's take a look at Gosar before we go."

Around a bend, the trees parted and the winding river dropped into a lush green valley of farmland. Scattered homes and landing platforms dotted the valley. At the far end, a city came into view at the foot of a mountain with towers, domes and landing ports rising above the trees. Palace towers stood guard over Gosar from a high ridge. Rays of morning light reached out from behind hazy blue mountains and sparkled in the dew on towers and rooftops.

"Most of Treya used to be this green," Annie said with a sigh.

"The farmland of the Gosar valley was once recorded to be the most productive in the world," Chip reported as they sped over the fields and meadows. He had finally settled back into his periodic reports of mundane facts and seemed to be enjoying the flight.

The ancient road from Gosar castle twisted down, over the foothills and joined the main road through the city. She had often explored Gosar on imaginary missions for the mythical secret Guardians with Chip and Brandon. During those games they had discovered many back alleys and passages. Clearing the rooftops and weaving through the towers, their ship sailed down into the large open space of a city park.

Annie set the ship lightly down beside a grand fountain. The side door of the shuttle swung up, the steps lowered and she stepped out on the green lawn. A cascade of water-pools made of white stone followed a stream up the hill among flowering shrubs and trees. Water fell from pool to pool and re-circulated in a springing display of fountains. "This is one of my favorite spots. Come see the fish." She led Chip to the edge of the lowest pool.

Chip hesitated before leaning over the water. "I've never been close to a live swimming fish."

"I think they're fascinating." Annie looked down into the clear pool. A group of similar orange, yellow and turquoise fish glided through the pool while they investigated ripples on the surface. She reached down into the water and they scattered.

"End Game!" an electronic voice announced. Annie stood and took a last look at Chip.

"It was nice seeing you again, Chip, but our time is up. I'll see you around soon." Chip smiled after they tapped their fists together. He then raised his hand in farewell.

Annie pressed a button on her wristband and commanded, "End simulation!"

Everything went black.

Annie flipped up the dark visor on her helmet. E-Chip, her small round droid, hovered nearby in her bedroom. She placed the flight simulator helmet on a shelf. Her fingers ran across the letters spelling COMMANDER BRYAN ROESHELL. She had made good use of her father's old flight programs and had made some modifications of her own—like adding fish to the fountain.

"Master Jordan will arrive anytime now," Annie said with eager anticipation. "I hope you enjoyed your virtual flight, E-Chip."

No longer able to talk as the copilot, the flying droid flashed lights and bleeped in a snippy retort.

Annie knew E-Chip was programmed to protect her, and it rattled his electrons whenever he flew with her.

Annie wandered out onto her balcony high above the growing tropic city of Caldera. Her long gold hair swept back in a chilly breeze. She wrapped her arms around herself. The heated kingdoms along the Equator were havens to escape the spreading snowfields. People far below scurried through the crowded streets. Something small floated down and landed on her hand. White crystals melted on her skin.

"Snow?" It was the first snowflake she had ever seen in Caldera.

There was a hush in the air as people in balconies on other buildings also looked up. Scattered blossoms of ice drifted among the apartment towers to the streets below.

E-Chip hovered beside her while they watched the flakes grow in size and number.

"The snow has never come this far before," she murmured and went inside to curl up on a window seat. There was no hiding from the freezing world's bleak future. The growing storms threatened to return her home world of Treya to its frozen natural state as the ancient weather control satellite slowly failed. The dying power core came from the ancient ship of the first colonists, called the Firestar. The origin of the naturally formed orb was unknown and engineers didn't understand its processing of electro-magnetic plasma well enough to build a replacement.

All hope for the people of Treya was on the Starseeker missions to find new food sources. She pulled out a golden object on a cord around her neck as she often did when she was troubled. She ran her thumb over the smooth ring and the worn down insignia of seahorses. The feel of it was comforting and reminded her of her mother. It was the last thing her mother gave her before her parents left on a mission to Tamaroon when she was six. She felt protected somehow by its promise of their return. Closing her eyes, she held it in her hands and brought to mind a faded image of their faces. She felt both close and distant to their memory. She kissed the ring and dropped it back beneath her tunic.

They left me here all alone, she thought and looked longingly up beyond the clouds. Despite all the reasons she had heard, they *had* left her behind and she wanted more than anything to see them again. Why the star-trail charts to Tamaroon were missing from command was a mystery. It was as if some unknown force didn't want them found.

Sparkling rays poured down through the clouds onto bright spots of snow on the mountains and brilliant green patches of fields to the north. Farmland surrounded the city like a sea of green that rippled like ocean waves in the gusting breeze. Transportation pods in the city busily ran along a high web of rails between and through buildings. To most people, the chaotic city was a sanctuary for safekeeping. To Annie, her safekeeping felt more like a prison.

Shuttles were flying on curved laser paths to and

from high platforms above the growing city. Vectronic paths of the autopilot were usually invisible, but in the chilly morning mist among the tall buildings, laser beams reflected a rainbow of colors. *If only the path to Tamaroon could reveal itself in such a mist,* she mused gloomily.

A holovision of amusing creatures appeared by the window, accompanied by electronic bleeps.

"I'm Okay, E-Chip, Knock it off."

The little droid retracted his holo-projector, lowered his visual lenses and emitted a low sound like a sigh.

"I'm sorry Chip, there's no time for games."

Uncle Jordan had come to visit and his deep voice resonated from the next room. He sounded agitated as he spoke to her aunt. Annie held her breath and made her way to one side of the open doorway. E-Chip beeped behind her.

"Stay, E-Chip," Annie whispered. She leaned near the door to listen.

Uncle Jordan stood calmly before Annie's regal Aunt Constance. He was a fit, middle-aged man with gray temples. His long instructor's vest was caught behind the laser gun at his waist. A dark blue Starseeker uniform sectioned off by flowing gray lines was beneath it.

Uncle Jordan plied words of persuasion upon her Aunt. "Her parents launched on their return mission to Tamaroon six years ago. We know well that the chance of their return is slim to none."

Once again grief over her parents stabbed through Annie's thoughts. Her chest squeezed tight and made it hard to breath. *They don't know! My parents could be alive, and need help to get back.* Sorrow passed and the voices in the next room again drew her attention.

"Precisely why, as her guardian, I should decide what is best for her. Angelina is only twelve years old and couldn't possibly be considered. This blasted ice age has turned the whole world upside down." The piercing dark eyes of her aunt looked at her uncle past the prominence of her nose. Her blonde streaked hair swept gracefully up like a crown. Her lavender gown of swirling crystals, draped regally to the floor. Constance always seemed to enjoy telling people what to do, but it never worked too well with Master Jordan. He could somehow always convince people to do what he said was best for the common good.

"Starseeker training would be the best thing for her. She has all the information her parents left on her study station. You know her parents would have wanted her to do this. Annie thinks of nothing but the Starseeker Corp. Besides, you said she was becoming a discipline problem – something about leaving and running about without permission."

Annie scowled in the next room as she pressed her ear closer to the door. Aunt Constance had no good reason why she shouldn't be allowed to explore the city below. What could possibly happen to her in the public data center, an art gallery or a local guild shop? She sometimes felt smothered by her aunt's overprotective rules.

"Fine! Take her to apply for the Corp at the castle. They most likely won't accept her anyway, despite your unwavering determination." Aunt Constance turned with her head held high and strode with regal grace to her private rooms. Uncle Jordan turned to find Annie standing in the doorway. He smiled, and his eyes grew wide with excitement.

"Well, young lady! How would you like to take a trip with me to a castle?"

Life with Aunt Constance had taught her that grand hopes were out of her reach, but Master Jordan made anything seem possible. He had often said that as her father's best friend, it was his duty to check in on her often. No matter the reason, she was always eager to go anywhere with him.

"The test is in one of the northern cities at Gosar castle, isn't it?" Annie asked, giddy with excitement. She knew the answer, but she often toyed with her conversations with Uncle Jordan.

"Yes, not only is it a northern kingdom, it is the central kingdom. I'm sure you remember that Gosar is the home of King Olsgood. He is the one king that rules the council of all the kings on Treya. He is also the one who put an end to all war so we could work on surviving the rapid fall into an ice age."

"The central kingdom? Isn't that where the

princesses dance with the newly crowned prince heir of Gosar?" Her face was bright with excitement.

Uncle Jordan laughed and gave her a hug, "Yes, let's go see where the princesses dance."

In no more than ten tarpecs, they left wearing light thermal capes. Annie was nervous to face the unknown but she was eager for it. The trans-tube doors suctioned the vacuum compartment closed.

Uncle Jordan scanned his hand on the security pad by the door. "Take me to my ship, please." The vacuum tube carried them to the secured launch bay where his ship had been stored. His shuttle was a sleek compact mini-jet. They boarded, and he locked in the auto-pilot destination.

The traffic tower responded, "Your destination has been received. You are clear for launch." Thrusters fired up and shot the shuttle out the side of the tall building.

Annie vaguely remembered being afraid to fly so high above the streets. She marveled at the soaring birds flying with them through the open air among the towers. The Caldera autopilot, smoothly guided the shuttle to the edge of the city where it was released. Annie sat quietly next to her uncle. He saw her eye the controls while setting their course for Gosar. When they flew together, he would often turn the controls over to her—but today was different. She was on her way to take the recruiting test for the Starseeker Corp.

"There's no time for side trips today," he said. "You need to concentrate on the test."

Flying north, they left the solar cell rooftops of the tropics, and the outdoor temperature reading dropped quickly on the panel overhead. They flew over turbo dams next to fish farms and the lonely towers of decaying nuclear reactors. The landscape below them was soon a rippling white sheet of snow in every direction.

"The snow is pretty, but it looks so empty," Annie said.

"Compared to how crowded it is where you and your aunt live, it is. People abandoned the farms and moved to the central kingdoms because of the freezing temperature and spreading ice." Master Jordan was an instructor at the Starseeker space station and often treated Annie like a student.

His special attention made her grin, and she couldn't sit still. She often played at impressing him with something he hadn't taught her. A spark of excitement shot through her mind when she remembered something she had read. "The central kingdoms are where they built those really big buildings mostly underground where lots of people can live. They used things that we throw away to make them."

"Ah yes," her uncle smiled at her familiar game. "The garbage huts. You really can't tell by looking at them. The thick walls insulate against cold and sound."

Annie twisted about in her seat. "Mom grew up in the kingdom of Nethas. Will we see it?"

"No, I'm afraid not. The kingdom of Nethas is far to the east. Your mother's parents didn't approve of your father taking her into space." His grin formed a tight line when he looked at Annie with concern.

Annie knew Uncle Jordan didn't like talking about her grandparents so she didn't press the subject. "Aunt Constance didn't sound too happy about me joining the Starseekers."

"I think it's because your Uncle Ben was always away on missions and because of his fatal mission years ago. She doesn't care much for the Corp. Many improvements have been made since then. Constance may disapprove but she knows, as I do, that the Starseeker Corp is the best place for you." Uncle Jordan looked down at Annie. "You know this is what your parents wanted for you, Annie. You've been studying for years now."

"I know," she said, as she twisted her hands about in her lap. "But what if I don't pass the test?"

Uncle Jordan smiled, "You know everything you need to know. I wouldn't have requested Starseeker training if I didn't think you were ready. Even if you don't do well on the test you can always try again next year."

Annie felt some relief, but her stomach remained hollow and tight. She did want to be a Starseeker but she wanted even more not to disappoint Uncle Jordan.

Rugged rows of massive mountains loomed ahead. It wasn't long before their ship was weaving its way among the white peaks beneath the high clouds. A high snowfield full of tall grey paddle fans passed below them. The speed of the huge blades varied with the gusting frigid air.

Master Jordan pointed a finger towards them. "That is one of King Olsgood's new wind farms." The shuttle dipped down into the next valley. "He also buried pipes deep in this valley to harvest steam to heat the greenhouses."

Annie imagined a maze of pipes deep underground. In her mind she could see the vast web of small tunnels feeding a channel under the city to bring warmth to growing crops and people working in a frozen land.

Dark shapes at the base of a mountain grew as their ship flew over the valley. The Gosar kingdom was shielded from the frigid air by a large clear dome. Another shuttle flew into the city through the wall of the giant bubble. Annie sat forward on the edge of her seat. "Is that an energy dome?"

Master Jordan simply smiled and nodded. "The shield built by engineers from Nethas can control what passes through, the temperature inside, and if necessary, protect the city from attack."

Monorail tracks fanned out from the city like the ribs of a fan to windowless apartment buildings, factories and smaller domes shielding the greenhouses.

Beyond the central dome, an ancient castle crowned the top of a high mountain ridge in a globe of its own. Its towers rose over the city rooftops that hugged the rise and fall of the rocky foothills. Wide walkways, made of white stone, wove between buildings and followed the contours of the land. Crowded rows of colorful shops with shaded fountain courts and plazas lined the streets. Grassy hills with planting beds, flowered among the buildings and walkways. It all looked so wonderfully strange surrounded by the drifting snow outside the dome.

"Wow!" Annie leaned forward to look down on the city. "It's even better than the pictures on the data stream." She was used to the simulator version her father created before there were domes or snow in the green valley of Gosar.

Uncle Jordan smiled. "Seeing the real thing is always more impressive." A list of destinations cascaded onto a holoscreen floating in the zebidon mist before them. The Gosar autopilot had locked on to their ship. Master Jordan tapped in a selection and released the pilot controls on the touch pad.

The shuttle slowed into a swooping path toward the castle. The ancient marbled stone fortress was the largest in the world. Royal blue and gold flags flew above the towers that reached up toward the clouds heavy with snow above the invisible shield. Windows in the stone towers looked out on the surrounding land. A glass dome held in an intricate lace of metal protected the central courtyard.

"Landing sequence engaged," a pleasant voice announced. The shuttle hovered gently down among the towers to the rooftop-landing pad.

Uncle Jordan took Annie's hand and smiled. "Welcome to Gosar!"

2

GOSAR KINGDOM

TOWERS REACHING TO THE SKY and ancient battlements surrounded the rooftop shuttle port. Royal guards watched over the many new arrivals passing through the palace entry. Annie and Uncle Jordan followed the others to the steward's gateway. Annie stopped before the steward and held out her hand to be scanned on a data pad. But her uncle quickly took her hand in his left hand and placed his right on the scanner. "Master Jordan Tarsynius of Gosar, tutor to Prince Garret and Prince Gregory" the electronic pad announced.

"Welcome, Master Jordan." The steward nodded his head.

Jordan then introduced Annie. "This is one of my students, Annie Roeshell. She is here to take the Starseeker test for the first time."

"Oh, I see!" The steward regarded Annie with a

curious expression. He waved them on into the palace.

Jordan brushed quickly past the entry guards with Annie in tow.

Annie sensed Uncle Jordan was hiding something. "Why didn't they scan my hand?"

Jordan stopped to bend down to her with his finger to his lips "Not now," he winked. He stood back up with his eyes full of excitement. "Are you ready to see the palace?" He gave a short bow and extended his hand to point the way ahead. The smile on his face was so big Annie couldn't help but become excited.

Marble-winged horses mounted by ancient knights with swords stood guard over the large entry hall. Stone planters spilled over with lush green foliage and colorful sprays of flowers from the mountains. But it was nothing compared to the grand central hall of the castle. Tall white doors trimmed with gleaming gold opened to a vast room with white marble floors. Their footsteps and the voices of others echoed in the enormous room.

Uncle Jordan began talking to some men she didn't know, so she drifted to one of the many couches neatly arranged around the tall pillars and sat down. The soft blue patterned cushions and carved wooden furniture were grander than she had ever seen before. Water splashed and jumped playfully as it performed a dance in the central fountain among tall pillars topped with trailing clouds of delicate flowers.

Annie's gaze traveled up the rows of columns to the carved vaulted ceilings high above her. Thousands of glittering crystals hung down like twinkling stars. The enormous room made her feel very small.

"Hello!" Annie jumped at the sudden greeting from a girl she suddenly found sitting beside her. Short spiky black hair flipped about and framed her dark eyes, fair skin, and warm smile. "Hi, I'm Melody. I didn't mean to scare you. What's your name?" An excitement shone in her bright expression.

"Oh," Annie croaked in surprise. "I'm Angelina! But most people call me Annie."

"Are you here for the Starseeker test?" Melody asked.

"Yes," Annie said. Melody's open friendliness was welcome in the unfamiliar palace.

"I thought I was young compared to the rest of the kids here." Melody said after she glanced about. "You look even younger than I am. I'm fourteen years old. How old are you?"

"I'm twelve," Annie said. "But I'll be thirteen soon."

Melody looked about at the other young faces in the room. "I hope they're not all *brainiacs* or we don't stand a chance."

Annie hadn't really noticed the others before. They did look older. Some of them standing in groups looked much older -- and most of them were boys.

One boy with dark hair looked back at them with

a disagreeable glare and made Annie uncomfortable. "Why would girls taking the test bother him?"

"Oh, don't mind him," Melody said. "Gillo Sarvok is the prince of one of the small kingdoms. His uncle took over after his parents died. Mom says they're all a bunch of snobs that think they are better than anyone else. Dad calls them rebellious rebels because they don't like being told what to do."

Annie saw a tall lean figure with a familiar face and a huge smile of large white teeth. She felt the tug of her own smile as he came near. They had not met often in the last few years. Ever since she moved to Caldera, they had only met in the simulator to play Guardian missions and fly shuttles. He crossed the room quickly to where they sat.

"Brandon, I didn't know you would be here."

"You're kidding me. My dad has been pumping me for this test since I was born." Today as usual, Brandon was a beaming ball of enthusiasm beneath his shaggy mop of reddish brown hair. He sprawled across the end of the couch beside Annie. He looked truly *hypertronic* with excitement radiating from every pore. His black and yellow jumpsuit full of zippers had the collar flipped up like he was ready to fly. Brandon could at times even look handsome, but Annie mostly thought of him as a playful puppy.

"Melody, this is Brandon. His dad used to pilot my dad's space ship."

Brandon frowned. "Well yeah, but Dad's also the

chief shuttle mechanic on the Starseeker station."

"I didn't know that," Annie said in surprise.

"Sure, sure! My mom and I have been living up there for years now. It's the coolest place. You'll love it up there."

Brandon would love it anywhere as long as he got to fly a space ship, Annie thought. She was glad to see Brandon again. On the Starseeker station, he had been like a brother to her before her parents left on their mission.

"Well, it's almost time for the starting bell. I better get back to the folks. I'll see you two later!" When he had disappeared in the growing crowd Melody looked at Annie with a smile.

"He's cute! Is he your boyfriend?"

"No he's just a friend. He's almost like a brother."

Melody's smile grew even bigger. She fidgeted for a moment and stood, "Well, I better go back to my parents too, where's yours?"

"Oh, I—don't have any" Annie glanced away. "I'm here with my teacher, Master Jordan."

"Oh, I'm sorry." Melody looked away as her cheeks burned red with embarrassment. "I hope to see you after the test. Good luck!" She smiled sincerely, waved and was gone. Uncle Jordan then came out of the crowd and sat beside her.

"It looks like you found a few friends."

"That was Brandon and a girl named Melody."

"Melody Turnhurst—I know her father. He's an engineer on a starship."

"I swear, Uncle Jordan, you know everyone."

"No, I don't know everyone." He chuckled and checked the time on his wristband. "It's about time for the test. Don't be nervous. I know most of them are older than you, but I know you'll do well." Now Annie *was* nervous. She knew all the others had high pod scores or they wouldn't have been granted entrance to the test. Her aunt said she was too young and now she knew why. Bells chimed by the doors to the king's council room for the test. A somber man in a royal uniform made the announcement."

"Ladies and gentlemen, you may now enter and find a seat at a study pod."

The Starseeker candidates entered a spacious room with a high ceiling. Rows of study terminals had been temporarily set up in the amphitheater of the king's council. The upper gallery was silently empty. The names of the twelve kingdoms were carved in marble and above the podium were the words *One council and all prevail.*

They were soon all seated in small booths shielded from each other by low walls.

"You may now begin," a voice announced.

Holographic touch screens appeared in the air before them. Questions with video images of moving plant cells, animals and star constellations flashed by as they clicked through the test.

Annie was afraid the questions would be too hard. She nervously clicked through the first few questions.

As she worked, she was surprised that most of them seemed easy. Her mind methodically ticked through the familiar calculations and digi-pics. The test covered many subjects and it took her two tarens to complete. Annie had an unsettled feeling as she was leaving and looked back at the others.

She wasn't the first one to leave the room but she wasn't the last one either. Students submitted their work with a final tap on the screen and left to wait in the lobby for the results to be announced.

The test shouldn't have been so easy. Did I get caught by trick questions?

Uncle Jordan stood up and greeted her with a big smile. "Now that wasn't so bad, was it?"

"I think I did all right," Annie said with a worried frown.

Melody waved to her from one of the couches. She was sitting with a couple dressed in Starseeker uniforms."

"Can I go see how Melody did?"

"Of course you can. I'll wait here with the parents." It made Annie smile to think that Uncle Jordan might think of himself as her parent. She swiftly made her way through the milling crowd over to her new friend. Melody jumped up to meet her and was talking before she even got there.

"That test was so hard. I hope I didn't rush through it too fast. How did you do?"

"It wasn't too bad. I think I did all right." Melody

introduced Annie to her parents. Her mother was a medical assistant and her father was the chief engineer on a Starseeker ship. Their beaming smiles reflected the pride they had in their daughter. They sat holding hands and nervously waited for the results. Annie felt a wishful tug at her heart.

"I haven't seen Brandon yet," Melody said after searching the crowd. "Do you think he's okay?"

"I'm sure he's okay. I don't see him, either." Annie thought it odd how concerned Melody seemed for someone she had just met. They went to wait near the test room doors. A short time later, Brandon came out to join them. His *hypertronic* status had flipped to *lockdown* and he looked mad.

"Wow, I got so mixed up. I went back through and changed some of my answers. I hope I didn't blow it." He groaned and shoved his fists deep into his pockets. "My dad will blow a *fibbertron* if I don't pass." His face crumbled in agony. "I better go see him and Mom. Maybe I can soften the blow before the results are announced." His head hung from his drooping shoulders as he shuffled off and muttered, "I'm dead. I am so dead. My life is over as we speak."

"Poor Brandon!" Melody raised her clinched hands in worry. Agonized sympathy creased her brow.

Annie remained skeptical. She was used to Brandon's overblown dramatics so she wasn't sure how serious she should take his performance. "Maybe he did better than he thinks," Annie offered.

Melody responded hopefully "You're right, we still haven't heard the results."

A few more worried faces came out of the test room. When the last student returned to the grand hall, the results were automatically tallied. Annie returned to stand by Master Jordan. Trumpets sounded. The steward announced from the far end of the great hall. "The new cadets for the Starseeker Corp of Treya, will now be presented before his majesty King Olsgood." The assembly slowly funneled into the throne room and down a long broad stairway.

The throne room was almost as large as the grand hall. Light blue and gold banners spilled over the rails of two balcony levels from which a small group of dignitaries watched. The crowd was divided by the palace guards when they entered leaving the center of the floor open.

Trumpets sounded by a high platform of marble steps at the opposite end of the throne room. The royal family was announced by the steward.

"King Fynlon Olsgood, Queen Kyrahh and Prince Garret of Gosar." The royal family came smoothly forward from a doorway behind their thrones. Billowing blue robes trimmed in white fur studded with stones drifted regally from their shoulders. Jewel-encrusted gold shot sparks of light from the crowns on their heads. The steward at the foot of the steps bowed to the king. Everyone bowed until the royal family sat on their thrones.

Annie curiously watched their smooth and deliberate entry. She couldn't get a good look at the prince, but he looked no older than his reported fourteen years of age. The finely tailored royal garments made Annie notice that most of the students and their families were also dressed exceedingly well. She fidgeted as she felt acutely aware of her common appearance and lowly station.

What am I doing here? she thought and clung to Master Jordan's hand.

King Olsgood then raised his hand in greeting. His voice rang out clearly in the hushed room. "Congratulations to all who have today been accepted into the Starseeker Corp. The rest of you I hope will return next year better prepared. We need all of you who have the courage to face the unknown and risk your lives for the people of Treya. Steward, let us not delay." The steward turned and began. A zebidon information board began to glow in midair above the grand hall entry. It would soon reveal the names and faces of the new cadets.

"The new cadets accepted into Starseeker training are . . . ." One name after another was announced by the steward. The smiling new cadets hugged family members and then joined the formation in the center of the floor. Melody jumped at the announcement of her name. Annie saw her parents lovingly embrace her and try to shush her excited chatter. The list grew longer. Brandon's name was finally called. Enormous relief spread across his face after his dad slapped him on the back and shook his hand. The list of names had stopped. Annie's heart felt heavy in her chest. She hadn't passed the test after all. Uncle Jordan placed a comforting hand on her shoulder. A commotion rose after the steward turned to talk with other officials on the platform. He returned after a short discussion to stand before the crowd.

"Sorry for the delay." The steward cleared his throat. "The same high score was recorded by Gillo Sarvok and Celia Larsson." The boy with black hair, she had seen earlier, and a smartly dressed girl strode up to receive a metal pin of merit from the steward. Annie swallowed down a lump of sorrow and applauded with the others as they joined the new cadets in formation, but her heart was not in it and her eyes began to burn. She had never felt more distant from her parents than at this moment.

"The highest score" the steward continued, "was recorded by our youngest cadet, Annie Roeshell." Applause began. "Will Annie Roeshell step forward please?" Annie's hands went to her face in disbelief. It took Uncle Jordan's guiding hand on her shoulder to get her moving forward.

"That's you, Annie," Uncle Jordan said with a big grin. The crowd parted to make way for her to pass when they started to clap. The Starseeker Admiral Deker stood by the steward waiting to shake her hand. The admiral raised an approving eyebrow at Master

Jordan.

"Congratulations, young cadet." He fixed a small blue stone of honor on the front of her cape. Annie's face felt warm. She knew it had to be red from embarrassment. The admiral smiled kindly and signaled her to join the formation of new cadets. Gillo and Celia looked smugly down at her as she fell in beside them.

The king stood and spoke slowly. His words rang out again over the assembly. "Congratulations to our new cadets. May their efforts ensure the survival of our people." The queen and prince then rose and left with the king through a door behind their thrones.

Annie ran back to Uncle Jordan. He scooped her up in a big bear hug. Looking over his shoulder, Annie caught a glimpse of an elderly woman in a soft blue gown smiling at her from a dark balcony above. Annie looked back, but the woman was gone.

Uncle Jordan looked at her puzzled face. "Is something wrong?"

"Uh, no! It's nothing," she said. *Surely the lady in blue wasn't looking at me.*

3

PALACE GARDEN

PEOPLE STREAMED out of the lobby while Master
Jordan spoke briefly with the Starseeker Admiral.
Jordan's expression brightened when he returned to
lead Annie across the lobby and down a hallway to a
pair of tall doors.

"Before we leave, I have something to show you."
He scanned his hand beside the doors and they swung
open to the sound of falling water. "Some of the
discoveries from new planets are kept here in the
castle."

Annie found the soft light beaming down on the
courtyard fountain enchanting. The trees and shrubs
behind it were encircled by stone rails and crowned
above by a lacy dome. The cool air full of unfamiliar
scents made Annie shiver.

Master Jordan switched to instructor mode and
pointed out some of the interesting features of the new

discoveries. Some would change color or shape when touched. One even spit to capture insects in a trumpet of petals.

"Many of these new species were developed and germinated from plants collected on your father's first Tamaroon mission," Master Jordan told Annie. "The flowering Boannie shows great promise as a greenhouse crop, though there has been some trouble with fungus. Your father named it after you." He lifted one of the flowering branches.

Annie examined the stripes of violet that faded out onto white petals.

Uncle Jordan slipped out of instructor mode and smiled. Her curiosity seemed to please him. "This flower he named the Boannie. Did your father ever tell you that?"

"No—maybe—I don't remember." A twinge caught in her chest.

Annie's downcast eyes made Uncle Jordan change the subject. He always seemed to know when she didn't want to talk about her parents.

"The space station maintains all the plants and animals collected from missions for study. I'll make sure you're familiar with them before your final year on the station."

Pounding feet and a squeal of laughter then burst into the room from a doorway among the arches surrounding the covered courtyard. A small six year old boy scampered across the stone floor and was about to climb over the railing when he caught sight of them. He instantly stood soberly at attention. "Good day, Master Jordan."

"Good day, Your Highness," Master Jordan replied with a short bow. Uncle Jordan glanced at Annie with an amused expression. "Prince Gregory, I would like you to meet one of my students, Annie Roeshell."

Annie curtsied as her aunt had taught her.

"Prince Gregory is also a student of mine."

"It is a pleasure to meet you, Miss Roeshell." Prince Gregory nodded. "Please pardon my intrusion. We seldom have visitors in the courtyard."

Annie found the tumble of formal pleasantries from the small child amusing. His lines sounded well rehearsed and she imagined he often had to excuse himself from intruding on others.

"If you will excuse me now, I will leave you with your instructor." He nodded in a very proper fashion to Master Jordan. "Good day, sir." Gregory was ready to make good his escape when Jordan caught him.

"Prince Gregory!" His instructor's commanding words snared him.

He reluctantly turned back to Master Jordan. "Yes, sir?" Gregory no longer had any rehearsed lines and was now just a child with his teacher.

"Are you and Prince Garret playing hide and seek again?"

"Yes, sir," the boy glanced away knowing he was

caught.

Master Jordan looked sternly down upon him. "You know the trouble you got into last time with the cook."

Prince Gregory glanced at Annie with a sheepish smile. "Yes, sir. We're not going near the kitchen and all the off limit places—Mom and Dad's room and the lab . . . ."

"Very good," Master Jordan kindly approved. "I'll see you and your brother tomorrow, so get your studies done. Scoot along now or Garret will catch you for sure."

"Yes, sir. Thank you, sir." Gregory smiled gratefully and began his retreat to the arches, "Our studies are done or Garret wouldn't play." He waved and sidestepped into a run.

An older boy burst onto the balcony level above the door where Gregory made his exit. Garret scanned the garden below. His eyes grew wide with surprise when he saw Master Jordan.

"Master Jordan, Good day to you, sir." Garret gave Jordan a short nod with his hands behind his back. "Have you seen my brother Gregory, sir?"

Uncle Jordan pointed to the doorway opposite to the one Gregory had taken.

Garret smiled happily, but then cocked his head and frowned. Garret seemed to know that Master Jordan never gave you an answer to a question so easily.

Annie grinned when she guessed what he must be thinking.

Garret then pointed under the balcony with a questioning expression.

Jordan just nodded.

Garret gave a short stiff bow to Master Jordan and his guest. "Pardon the intrusion," He smiled mischievously and was off after his brother.

"Do they always act that way?" Annie asked.

"No," Uncle Jordan mused. "I believe we caught them off guard." They both laughed.

Annie thought it strange that royal princes could actually seem like normal people. She then remembered something important. "You didn't show me the ballroom yet. You know—where the princesses dance."

"Oh yes!" Uncle Jordan said in a playfully serious manner. "You already saw it."

Annie scrunched her face up in confusion.

Jordan grinned at what must have been a perplexed look on her face. "The ball is held in the throne room," he explained.

"Oh!" Annie said and imaginary figures in the throne room began to swirl about wearing sparkling gowns in her head.

"Someday you may dance with the prince."

Annie looked skeptically up at Uncle Jordan. She greatly doubted that would ever happen.

Master Jordan's thoughtful features changed, as if

he said something he shouldn't, and blustered, "Well, it is getting late and we have a long flight home."

Annie frowned in disappointment. She had no desire to leave the beautiful palace but knew they must return home. She followed Uncle Jordan and left with one last look at the flowering Boannie of Tamaroon.

Someday I'll be the one traveling to other planets, Annie mused. She smiled at the idea of leaving Caldera. The Starseeker test was just the beginning. Four years of training would follow, with the final year spent on the space station. Annie's hope of finding her parents one day, kindled into life.

4

STARSEEKER TRAINING
STARSEEKER STATION 9010

ANNIE LAY DEAD asleep in her bunk until the repeating tones finally made her flinch.

"Up, up, up!" AMARIS barked from the wristband beside Annie's study station. A star-charting lesson still glowed on the monitor. In the corner, E-Chip bleeped into ready mode.

"Time to rise and shine!" AMARIS continued. The automated voice bounced off the bare walls of her sleep bay.

Annie waved her hand about and the annoying chatter cut off. She rose sluggishly to her elbows.

"Please report in fifteen tarpecs to deck twenty-one for physical training." AMARIS directed.

Annie squinted at the growing brightness in the room. Her mind slowly clicked gears into the present. After three years at Gosar Academy, she had adjusted to the routine of a cadet and moved to the Starseeker space station for her fourth and final year of training. The time for new recruits to be commissioned as officers was drawing near.

She rolled off the gel mat in a nightshirt and smoothed out the heat sheet. Her bunk quietly slid away into the wall. She stretched and walked through the holovision of stars she had been studying last night. The door of her sleep bay glided open and she entered the squad bay she shared with three cadets.

Celia and Tris sat with empty breakfast trays at a table bolted to the floor.

"Everyone knows a nobleman is coming to join our final exams," Tris chattered without heed of Annie's presence. "But, I heard it's the Gosar prince who's training to be a ship commander."

"I knew it," Celia declared with a gleam in her eye. "Only a royal could join our class right before exams." Celia had seen Annie enter the room but appeared to ignore her passing.

Celia had over the years referred to her as Little Jumpsuit Annie. Her arrogance betrayed that she felt Annie was no threat when it came to boys. Her eyebrow rose with a sly expression. "That's why I had all my uniforms cleaned and pressed. There's sure to be an opportunity."

"He is really cute," Tris confessed.

"Cute?" Celia exclaimed. "I saw him in person once and he is seriously sweet." Celia fanned herself with her fingers while she rolled her eyes.

Annie wanted to gag. If it wasn't one guy, it was another. *How do they find the time?* she wondered. Their training schedule was grueling. She had managed to slip around Celia to the water lock, and avoid her usual snide remarks. Thankfully, AMARIS was aware of the time needed by each individual to complete tasks; Celia and Tris were roused very early, while Annie enjoyed extra sleep. She returned to find the others had left and been replaced by a girl with spiky black hair and large dark eyes.

"Good morning, sleepy head!" Melody was always way too chipper at the break of dawn.

Annie yawned. "Morning, Mel," Annie's first words of the day reluctantly came out in a sigh. Late study nights made it hard to get going. She selected a button on the meal minder that promptly dispensed a breakfast drink. She chugged it down and stuffed the container into a vacuum tube. Annie's puffy eyes crinkled when she grinned. "I'll see you later in combat."

Melody gave her a mocking salute. "I'll be armed and ready."

Since she only saw Uncle Jordan in the classroom and on occasional trips, Annie was thankful she had her best friend, Melody, as a training partner. She returned the mock salute and went to her room to dress for her assigned morning exercise.

Annie's feet pounded beneath her and sweat dripped down her face as she strained for each agonizing breath. The stars of the Meridian galaxy shined brightly in the windows that flashed by. The echo of pounding feet that urged her forward grew louder behind her. The others were quickly gaining ground. No longer in control, her breathing became hard and ragged as the last of her speed was spent. The thunder of feet was upon her. Her time was up. Her pace slowed and the others passed on into the tunnel track for another lap around the station. A wireless bud in one ear continued to play something with a heavy beat to keep her on pace.

Annie's chest and shoulders heaved as she plodded off into the side port. She pulled a towel from the top of a post that allowed a fresh towel from inside to rise and take its place. She wiped away the sweat and walked through the weight room to cool down. Resistance weight lifting stations were everywhere. A double beep sounded and older members of the Starseeker Corp stopped and switched stations.

Annie tapped her wristband. "Laps complete," she reported.

"This concludes your morning exercise." AMARIS replied in her ear bud. After a pause for processing, she continued. "You have—rest and relaxation for the remainder of the morning session. Report," AMARIS paused again, "to deck nine at 900 tarens for ship maintenance, KRP kitchen routing and processing."

"Yes!" Annie exclaimed and punched the air. She pressed her wristband to start her favorite music. She was free for a time now to do what she pleased. She danced her way to a stack of illuminated cubicles. She retrieved a jumpsuit in her size that was swiftly replaced. The quick slide of sporadic beats on her headset carried her in rhythmic step to the shower bay.

As she stood in line, carefree lyrics echoed in her mind and a sense of freedom tingled down her spine. She stepped forward and grinned at the facial scanner when the light was blue and passed through the airlock to the shower bay. Emergency antigravity hand holds in doors, floors and ceiling were more numerous here than elsewhere on the station.

They better not pull an AG drill, she thought. *Floating out of a shower stall would be extremely embarrassing.* Blasting drier jets in the floor and ceiling hit a trainee entering beside her. His wide-eyed yelp made her smile. Jumpy newbie trainees were easy to spot.

Annie found a door with a blue light above it. The bay was busy with more than half of the stalls lit red. Inside the small stall, she placed her contact lenses into a case and fed her clothes to a vacuum tube in the wall. A clear door with a frosted middle hissed open and clicked shut behind her. The cool tubular chamber suddenly filled with blasting warm liquid from soap jets in the wall. Annie turned about with her arms over her head and the sweaty grime melted away.

"Oo^{Oo}-Oo-$_{oo}$-ooow!" The strange cry of the Newbie rang out through the shower bay.

Annie grinned and she recalled her entire class having the same reaction almost a year ago.

After the rinse cycle, the air suction jets kicked on. Her hair was blown dry straight above her and all trace of moisture blew away. The shower door hissed and she quickly pulled on the clean jumpsuit and turned to the mirror.

She twisted her long blonde hair into a wide headband. The tan face of a fifteen year old smiled at her from the mirror. She squinted unhappily at the odd blue-violet color of her eyes. Inserting brown colored lenses over them no longer felt awkward. Her aunt claimed they blocked FV rays that damaged her eyes. Annie could never prove her wrong and obediently continued to wear them. She replaced her ear bud and left humming a happy bouncing tune that blocked the thoughts of gloom and doom.

Annie took the trans-tube to deck seventeen promenade galley and found an open window seat with a view of the horizon. She watched the sea of stars in the night pass slowly by. Over the last year, the scene had become familiar but it still was an awesome sight. She flipped through news reports of food shortages, ice storms, and protests in small kingdoms on her datacom and found the Starseeker Missions board. There were still no Starseeker missions scheduled to launch. Master Jordan warned there wouldn't be any until after graduation, but she hoped they would have been posted by now.

She thumbed through screen pages of clothing and hairstyles. She sighed as she thought how shopping wasn't quite so interesting without Melody in hyper drive over new fashions. She found a sensible pair of rugged hiking boots fit to wear to any planet and ordered them in her size. Her quadmar account had grown since she rarely spent anything. A live report scrolled by in the news stream about refugees waiting in line for living space and food. It reminded her that she would still be supplied with everything she needed while away on Starseeker missions while others "on-world" went without. She sent a large donation to the refugee fund, closed her datacom and took into her memory the view of her world that she would soon leave behind.

At 900 tarens, Annie made her way to the KRP loading docks.

"Blue totes first!" The dock master directed. Cold food items from the blue totes were loaded first in the refrigerated section. Room temperature items could wait. The dock crew pulled floating pallets off the transport ship and dropped them in the food routing room. Annie joined the others and took a crate to a wall of numbered slots.

She remembered being amazed at how her meals had magically appeared from the food dispensers on the ship. It wasn't so magical now, but it was still amazing.

When Annie ran into other cadets during ship maintenance, she always tried to be open and friendly. Today she only ran into Tris and Gillo. They both seemed to think manual labor and most people were beneath them so they responded with a typical raised chin and cast down look when she greeted them.

After KRP duty, Annie needed to see a friendly face. She had enough spare time to jump on the tube up to the kitchen on deck twenty-two and visit Brandon's mom. Mirra Granger served the head chef who cooked meals for the officers. She was chopping vegetables when Annie found her.

"Hi Mirra, could you use some help?" Annie found a knife and began chopping beside her.

"Annie dear, how are you?" Lines around Mirra's eyes crinkled with an affectionate smile before she gave her a hug.

"I'm fine," said Annie. "Brandon and Melody are almost done with modifications on the T35 Phantom. We should be able to take it for a test run any day." Annie's eyes opened wide with excitement. "Annnd—a new mystery cadet pilot entered the race."

Mirra shook her head. "I do hope you kids don't get into trouble so close to graduation."

Annie scraped the chopped vegetables into a bowl. "We're not doing anything wrong—not really. We've just arranged flight time for a number of us all at the same time—that's all."

Mirra sighed with worry and turned back to her work.

Annie continued to build her case. "Tad is the chief shuttle bay engineer and he doesn't think there's too much trouble we can get into. He wouldn't have agreed to help with the shuttle race if he thought his son would get in trouble."

"Oh, he didn't agree to anything, except to keep his mouth shut." Mirra flustered about. "I'll swear that I don't know anything, so don't tell me anymore about your crazy plans. I just hope no one gets hurt." She then turned the topic back to Brandon. "Tell me Annie, has that thickheaded son of mine shown any interest in Melody yet."

"No," Annie said with a groan. It was an age-old question Mirra would ask, especially when she wanted to change the subject. "Brandon just has a hard time expressing himself when it comes to anything serious. We all know he must like her." Annie crunched down on something that looked like a carrot.

"I know," Mirra conceded. "It's just that Melody is such a lovely girl. But they are still young and it isn't like I want to push things. I'm just interested in how they are getting along."

Annie laughed. "Well if it helps—they do seem to be spending more time together." Mirra perked up at this. "But," Annie continued, "It may just be because they're both working on the T35 together." Mirra scowled.

"Oh, go on and get out of my kitchen," Mirra said. "I'm sure you have something better to do." Annie grinned when Mirra shooed her off with the wave of a dish towel.

Annie checked AMARIS on her wristband. "Report to deck twenty-one at 12:00 tarens for combat training." That left more than enough time to eat lunch. Annie decided to stop by the shuttle bay on her way to the dining hall. She was hoping to run into Brandon and Melody.

The launch bay with the T35 was deserted. She left through a small door leading to the central hangar to check the repair shop. Entering the enormous storage and repair hangar she stopped to scan the ships being repaired for any sign of Melody, Brandon or his father Tad.

"Did you lose something?" a friendly yet unfamiliar voice asked from behind her.

Without turning around, Annie responded. "More like someone than something." She turned around to find a very handsome young man with dark hair laying on a stack of storage crates. He was wearing an old t-shirt cut short at the chest, sweat pants, and wristbands and seemed to have nothing to do.

"A boyfriend I suppose?" His easy smile was friendly.

"No, just a couple of friends that seem to have disappeared into thin air." Annie felt herself smiling but couldn't stop.

The stranger laughed. "I have the exact same problem with a couple of guys I know."

"I haven't seen you around before," Annie hedged. A sudden bout of shyness made it hard to think. "Are you a pilot or a trainee?"

"No," the stranger smiled thoughtfully as he looked into her eyes. He then glanced over at the ships in the hangar. "I would like to fly on a mission into space one day. But, I'm just here visiting. I'm checking things out you might say." His steady gaze held hers so completely it took her breath away before his attention shifted to two men grinning a short distance off. "Ah, there would be *my* two friends." He rose and started towards them. "It was nice meeting you—uh!" He looked at her waiting for a response. Annie felt strangely dazed.

"A-Annie, my name is Annie," she said.

He grinned. "It was nice meeting you, Annie, I hope I'll see you again." He gave her a short nod and was gone.

Annie stood for a moment reviewing in her mind what had just happened. *My name is A-A-Annie? How stupid he must think I am.* It then hit her, she never found out his name. *Who was that?* she groaned. I *just met the perfect guy and he thinks I'm a basket case.* She then noticed Melody waving from the repair shop and went to join her.

"The modifications are almost complete," Melody reported with an intense grin. Her expression changed when she noticed Annie's disturbed look. "Who were you just talking to?"

Annie's face immediately flushed and her words fell out in tumbled confusion. "I don't know. He was just—there—, when I came in. His name? His face seemed familiar—did you see him?" Annie was so rattled she couldn't think straight. Melody grinned. It was perfectly clear why her best friend was talking in circles.

"No, I couldn't see him from here. Was he cute? What did he say?"

A jumble of emotions played across Annie's face while she tried to tell Melody what just happened.

Brandon came out of the repair shop. "Let's go," he said and he walked quickly past them on his way to the dining hall. When he saw Melody and Annie following on his heels he fell back beside them. "We need to grab something to eat before we go rehearse how to pummel alien attackers." Brandon's face gleamed as he took a few playful jabs at Melody.

A thought made Melody suddenly sober. "They don't seriously think we'll ever need to—do they?" Melody looked at Annie.

"No," Annie said. "No alien beings have ever been discovered. They just want us to be able to defend ourselves. It's a military thing."

"Yeah, right!" Brandon said, and rolled his eyes. "It's all just pretend."

After lunch, they took the trans-tube to the combat gym on deck twenty-two. AMARIS was rotating other crewmembers through their assigned practice in weapon defense. Station numbers were marked on the cushioned floor. Practice light swords were stored in racks by the door. Annie, Melody and Brandon each selected a neutronic practice sword and joined their class in formation to one side of the floor.

Class always began with sword drills standing opposite their partners. Master Casbar led them in every thrust, flip and roll by calling out the required moves. He was as tough as the tuwesian granite that was fabricated for ancient battlements. He stalked along the row of cadets with keen, hawkish eyes, catching every missed move. The dodging rolls and flips grew more difficult as the exercise progressed.

At the end, Casbar walked the line and barked out which move each cadet needed work on. The ultimate defeat was when he had AMARIS assign a private session with him. They were all familiar with these grueling sessions.

"Be seated," Casbar directed. "Gillo Sarvok, front and center." Gillo, like his uncle, King Kretus Sarvok, was known to be a good swordsman. He was often chosen to help demonstrate the lesson for the day. He had dark hair and a scar on his left cheek.

"Today you will learn some disarming tactics." Casbar announced. He illustrated several different ways of forcing a weapon from an opponent's hand.

AMARIS reshuffled the pairing of the cadets to work on weak areas identified by Casbar. Annie found herself standing opposite Celia and they nodded stiffly to each. After the disarming drills, they performed a drill dictated by AMARIS in their ear buds designed to strengthen their weak areas. Light swords bounced and sparked off each other. The practice swords radiated a charge that sent an annoying buzzing sensation through nerves when the beam penetrated through an opponent. After Annie had been buzzed a number of times, the drill was ended and the first free fights began with the same partner.

Next to Annie and Celia, Brandon sparred against Gillo Sarvok. Most cadets avoided the sullen aristocrat. He seemed resentful at having to study with those beneath him, but he enjoyed working with a sword. His only weakness was an aggressive head-on attack that would throw him off balance. Brandon liked any challenge and threw himself into the battle with reckless enthusiasm.

Annie and Celia both felt no real need to exert themselves. Like some who had broken off engagement to watch others battle, Annie and Celia watched Brandon's aggressive "play" attack while Gillo calmly defended against every stroke.

Gillo went on the attack. He easily pressed Brandon with every stroke back to the line marking the edge of their practice area. Gillo stopped his press, smiling, a rare thing to see on his face. Gillo returned to the center mark of the drill mat and smirked to those that might be watching.

On his way to meet Gillo, Brandon suddenly waged a head-on attack with a flurry of crazed flickering beams aimed at Gillo's eyes and knocking him to the ground. Titters of laughter came from onlookers nearby.

"The great Gillo forced flat on his back, that's a first!" Celia taunted. Her cutting remark made Annie's anger flare. She glared first at Celia and then at Brandon.

"That wasn't fair," Annie chastised Brandon. She went to Gillo's side and extended a hand to help him up. "Sorry, he can be such a crazy animal sometimes." Gillo hesitated before taking Annie's hand. They stood briefly face to face. His gaze down on her was unreadable. Gillo turned and walked off in the awkward silence that followed. Melody came over and stood beside Annie.

"I can't believe you did that," Melody said.

"Brandon wasn't fighting fair. You can't do that with a real neutron sword." Annie looked away and caught a critical gaze from a young man in grey. His looked back to the sparring match he and others were watching.

5

SWORD FIGHT

THE CLASH OF SWORDS drew a growing group of onlookers. Celia, Tris and others curiously crossed to the other side of the gym to watch.

Brandon joined Annie and Melody and defended his actions. "I just took what advantage I could."

Annie felt like she was scolding her unruly brother. "Desperate acts like that are for when you're fighting for your life. Here you're supposed to learn how to use a neutron sword." Brandon saw her point and shrugged. Melody was anxious to change the subject.

"Let's go see who's fighting," Melody said, and slipped her hand into Brandon's to pull him along. Annie followed along behind them. They joined in with the onlookers now hemming in the sides of the rectangular practice quadrant. A younger student appeared to be getting direction from an older one.

They were both strong but the older one was larger. While most of their movements were familiar, some were obviously advanced. This prompted curious whispers among those watching. The younger player in the match now seemed annoyed by the number of people watching. It was then that Annie recognized him. He was the stranger she met in the shuttle bay.

"Forget them! Eyes here!" the older one directed and maneuvered for the advantage. "Curt, join us—the class would enjoy a demonstration of some advanced two on one."

The young student lowered his guard in a pleading objection. "Please Rick, not now." The older one, named Rick, just smiled and the stranger in gray joined in the fight. The younger swordsman threw off his exasperation and all three hunched into movements of a serious nature.

Sparks flew with the rapid exchanges. Their disregard for the audience forced those on the sidelines to dodge the flying weapons. Rick and Curt attacked again and again, but their prey deflected, sliced and spun out of their reach. Finally, the young swordsman went on the offensive. Catching Curt open, he disarmed him. He then attacked the one in charge of the fight and with a flurry of hard blows; he tackled him and put a dagger to his throat.

"Who said you could use the dagger?" Rick objected.

"I did," the defiant young victor replied.

Curt laughed and gave them both a hand up to their feet. Rick and Curt both gave the young warrior a short bow. The young victor gave them a mere nod. They all smiled and turned to leave. The spectators had broken out in spontaneous applause over the forcefully decisive end of the match. The session was over and they all dispersed to carry out their evening assignments.

"Wow, that sure was something!" Brandon smiled with gleaming eyes while he flashed his practice sword about. Annie rolled her eyes with a smile.

"Boys and their toys," Melody mused and followed Brandon on his way to the door. Annie looked over at the trio of fighters. Their old t-shirts didn't hide the fact that they were all three handsomely built. She couldn't help wondering who they were and why the younger one she had met in the shuttle bay now seemed familiar. She knew she had seen his face before today. Curt glanced her way and the youngest one did also.

Embarrassed that she had been caught looking, Annie hurried to catch up with her friends.

Out of the corner of her eye, Annie spied a darkly dressed figure look at her and glance back at the swordsmen. It seemed that their exchange had not gone unnoticed. How long had he been watching them from the weapon racks and why did he look so curious at her? His gaze had unnerved her. *There is surely nothing special about the lives of two teenagers,* she thought and she blocked it from her mind.

Annie followed quietly behind her friends. The face of the young swordsman lingered in her mind. She recalled his smile from their first encounter that morning. Why did he seem familiar? Maybe it was because she replayed their first meeting so often in her thoughts.

It had been a long day and the dining hall was a welcome site. They scooped up some food from several food ports at one end of the hall. The maintenance crew was clearing tables and a new wave of dinners arrived. The trio headed for the same table they always used in the corner.

Melody looked at Brandon's heaping tray with disgust. "You should weigh three times what you do."

"I'm a growing boy." Brandon beamed. He enjoyed being in the spotlight. "How else am I going to put some beef on this rack?" He put his tray down and proudly pumped up his biceps for the admiration of all to see. "There's not an inch of fat on these puppies." Brandon looked at the two girls for some words of praise. "In the last month these goose eggs have really grown."

"I don't see any difference," Annie said. She knew she couldn't knock a hole in his playful pride.

Melody gave him a teasing jab in the side. "Sit down you big goof!"

"Oh, I'm hurt!" Brandon dramatically grabbed his side and acted out the pain of it all. "I need a band-aid," he feigned in a groan.

"A band-aid?" Melody asked. There had to be a punch line.

Brandon's face lit up at this, flashed a huge smile and flexed his arms into a pose. "Because I am cut." He was totally amused with himself.

Melody paused dumbfounded for a moment, but then broke into a laugh when she got it.

Annie smirked in a restrained smile. It was an old line from when they were young, but he could put on such a comical display that his antics never got old.

Annie and Melody shared a look and shook their heads, unable not to be amused.

Brandon's face went suddenly serious when he sat. He spread his hand out on the table and leaned forward. "So, who was the flashy guy defending against two swordsmen?"

Melody's mouth dropped. "Don't you know?"

"No, should I?" He looked back at Melody with wide-eyed sarcasm.

"Doesn't he even look familiar?" Melody loved toying with Brandon when she thought she knew something he didn't know. Usually this had to do with engineering specifications on, say, the amount of compression needed in the fastest star class engine core.

Annie didn't have patience for their juvenile banter. "Come on Mel, who is he?"

Melody looked at Annie with surprise. "You mean

you don't know either?"

"Would I be asking if I did?"

Melody sat with a stunned look on her face at both of them. "Boy, you two have really lived sheltered lives." Melody's expression softened. "He is *the* prince of Gosar, Garret Olsgood, the one that is going to be crowned the heir of Gosar in seven days."

It was Annie's turn to be stunned. All sound and time suddenly ceased to exist while this fact sank into her mind. She then came reeling back to her senses.

"Annie, Annie! Are you okay?" Melody's words echoed hazily as Annie came out of a fog.

"Hello-o!" Brandon waved his hand in front of her face. He pretended to have a microphone in his hand. "Testing, testing—is your receiver on line? She's not turning blue. I think she's okay!"

"But—it's him," she managed to get out. She looked directly at Melody. "He's the guy."

"What guy?" Brandon asked. He hated being left out, but wasn't sure if he wanted to know. "He's just some high-faluting royal."

Melody appeared to get the message. "Oh Annie, I'm so sorry."

"Sorry about what?" Brandon was now seriously concerned for his old friend.

Melody quietly put him off. "I'll tell you about it later." She refocused on Annie.

Annie had lost her appetite. She pushed her tray away and stood to leave. The joyous triumph of finally knowing his name was quickly erased by despair. He was a royal prince who was totally off limits to an orphaned nobody like her. She loathed the feeling of barely having a name for an identity.

Melody seemed to know she was in no condition to respond. "If you want to talk about it, let me know."

Annie left without a word. The flood of her thoughts surged to find some unseen glimmer of hope. *The prince of Gosar. who will one day rule the Council of Kings. Could I really be falling for the guy who would one day rule the entire planet?*

CINDERS OF ELLEN

DAY 2

ANNIE'S EYES reflected the bright burning hope of the stars as she gazed upward and beyond the clear dome overhead. The glistening white surface of Treya passed by as the space station continued to rotate. Annie wondered, *Is there any harm in pretending a prince might like me? I know it's an impossible fairytale romance and just a hopeless crush.* The star field passed slowly overhead and her thoughts strayed out among them. *It's also unlikely that Starseekers will find answers on a distant planet to save Treya.* A small satellite in a faster orbit floated quickly by and off into space.

Annie leaned against a tree inside one of the many large clear domes that formed a glowing crown at the top of the station. A ring of bright lights above her, shined warmly through the green leaves of the small forest. The light cycles in the planetary habitats varied, imitating its home world. Starseekers collected and tested new plants for growing food in a frigid and artificial climates. The isolation of the alien plants was necessary to protect the fragile world below from the unknown.

Annie whistled and searched the branches of the trees. The air inside the dome called the Cinders-of-Ellen, was cool, moist and clean. It echoed with the sounds of life from the planet Tamaroon. Wings fluttered and leaves rustled with the movement of small creatures.

I wonder where Tipper is? Annie yawned and noticed E-Chip poking about as usual on their morning inspection of the dome. He chittered and beeped at every minor encounter with creatures now light years from their home on Tamaroon. A rushing waterfall tumbled into a pool. Its surging waves lapped rhythmically along the black shore of cinders from the Ellen Sea.

Annie had not slept well. Thoughts of Garret clouded her mind while she performed her duties. On an upper quadrant of the great clear dome, Annie noticed a small robot was traveling in a halting zigzag.

"Uh-oh!" she said to E-Chip. "Scrubber-bot down."

She mounted a maintenance platform and closed the safety rail. It was a saucer shaped platform with a control column, housed in a portable maintenance booth. With a few bleeps and the flip of some switches, the platform slowly rose. She easily maneuvered it through the tree tops and brought it in reach of the robot. She detached the scrubber from the dome wall and plugged it into the diagnostic jack. The readout confirmed what she suspected.

"Like I couldn't have guessed." She held it up to a vacuum port and pressed the robot's eject button. A side port opened and a cloud of dust and grit shot out. "Flying sprockets!" she coughed. "How can you find all that on a ceiling?" She reattached the scrubber to the ceiling and descended, returning to the entry deck. Annie picked up a small tool pack and went back to her routine visual check.

Annie's hand caressed the trunks of the trees as she strolled over the soft moss and through the ferns. In six days, Garret would dance the royal waltz with the princesses. It was a dance her mother had taught her at the age of six. The tune hummed in her memory and the waltzing melody rose into a song on her lips. Small speckled birds gathered on a branch and twittered in response.

Annie laughed lightly. "Don't you like the way I sing? I suppose you think you can do better." One of the speckled birds piped its familiar call loudly in response. "OK, you crazy bird, you win." She laughed but suddenly sobered. "Oh my, I'm talking to birds. That can't be a good sign." She shrugged and laughed at herself.

She couldn't explain the blissful mood she was in.

The perfect guy had walked into her life and turned out to be a royal prince. He was royalty and her parents were not noblemen. She had no hope of even getting to know him. But, the mystery guy now had a name. Garret Olsgood. It had been many years since she felt this happy.

She sat among the flowering Boannie shrubs her father had named after her. She breathed in the sweet scent that reminded her of cherry almond scent that her mother often wore. It had been ten years since her parents left, and her heart often ached when she felt lost and abandoned. Memories of the last time she saw her parents came swirling back. Whirling images and voices from when she was six years old spun in her head . . . .

The blurred image of her mother suddenly sharpened. She could hear her mother's gentle voice. "Give me a hug, little angel." The image fuzzed and she heard an echo of her voice say— "We'll sing and dance again soon." The memory blurred and changed.

Her father's face appeared. He scooped her up in his arms. "Your mother is such a worry wart." He kissed and tickled her. In the fog of her memory, she saw her parents in each other's arms. "Jordan says we're still safe," her father's words resonated. "It's almost time to launch, we have to scoot!" his voice echoed. The foggy memory of two flying droids zapping each other became dancing colored beams of battling practice swords. The clashing colored beams sent sprays of sparks flying—thoughts of a handsome face ran through her mind.

Annie was caught by surprise and her mind jumped back to the present. "What is this?" she groaned.

E-Chip bleeped a response.

"Why can't I get this guy out of my head? There's no hope I'll ever get to know him. A prince could never consider a poor orphaned girl. He might as well live on the other side of the universe." She felt very alone sitting among the flowering trees from Tamaroon. She inhaled the scent of blooming flowers her father had named the Boannie. Thoughts spurred by her desire to go looking for her parents had ended with thoughts of a prince who was out of her league.

"Caw-ca-caw!" A bright blue bird with an orange bill and golden breast called from overhead. His speckled topknot sprung up with his excitement.

"Tipper, what are you fussing about?" she playfully scolded. "There is no one here except E-Chip and me."

A bright-colored bird fluttered to her knee and chirped happily.

"There you are! I've been looking for you everywhere, Tipper." She picked him up and stroked her little friend's feathers with her finger. "Have you been off napping somewhere?" Tipper and E-Chip were her constant companions in the dome.

The fine black sand made of cinders felt cool on her buried feet. The cinders had come to the space station with the plants from the shores of the Ellen

Sea. She looked up at the stars far beyond the dome.

"Uncle Jordan thinks rebels erased the Tamaroon records. But, just because Starseeker Command couldn't accurately record distant planet locations ten years ago, doesn't mean I can't dig up where you came from." How else would she ever find where her parents went? *"I'm going to find Tamaroon and my parents,"* she vowed to herself.

She rose and gently placed Tipper on a branch. "I'm almost done. Did you want to come home with me today?" Tipper responded with a chirp. He often hung out nearby while she worked. Annie's baggy old jumpsuit felt light but warm in the cool air. She rewound her hair and stuffed it back in her cap, put her sunglasses on and shouldered her tool pack.

Fluttering butterflies flew up from a dense row of shrubs when she passed out into the bright light. She stood on stones at the edge of a water pool that reflected the stars above. The ripples in the water lapped softly on the black sand at the edges of the pool. Annie's bare feet stepped from stone to stone across the top of the waterfall.

"Annie!" Master Jordan shouted.

Annie's heart jumped and her arms and legs waved wildly about in a struggle for balance. But, with practiced grace she managed to catch herself by using the weight of the tools.

Master Jordan smiled. She could see him by the doorway beyond the lower pool. His hand shaded his eyes from the bright lights above. The entry to the agriculture domes was restricted and her uncle's unannounced visits were always a surprise. E-chip floated by him where he guarded the door. *Some guard!* she thought. *I'll have to modify his program later.*

"You did very well on your exam yesterday. Don't stay too late—I'll see you in the lecture hall this evening." He raised a hand in farewell and carried away a small Boannie tree. The fruit bearing trees in greenhouses on Treya had developed a fungus and were being studied.

"Yes, sir!" Annie called back.

Tipper chirped in annoyance from a nearby tree. She then noticed that Prince Garret in a clean-cut uniform had followed the instructor and was squinting up at her with a furrowed brow. She quickly ducked behind the shrubs on the other shore. He looked both amused and perplexed before he left. How much he had seen or heard Annie didn't know.

7

CADET CLASSROOM

THE DOOR CLOSED BEHIND ANNIE before she opened the tool pack in her cabin. Tipper darted out to a dish of birdseed and chirped happily. E-Chip plugged himself into a wall port and bleeped.

"See if you can pick up on any news, Chip."

E-Chip clicked and emitted an assortment of tones. A message from E-Chip ran across the top of her podcom screen. "No leads on primary search," the message reported. "The cadet class will be visited by Prince Garret today."

After reading the message, Annie recalled the last look on Garret's face and winced. "No kidding. You're a bit late on that one." Annie sat in her floating chair, flipped through files on her podcom and opened her Tamaroon search file. She clicked on a link that returned her to a data stream search for the mysterious planet and her parent's mission. "Continue with primary search Chip." A small data dish on E-Chip twitched as it scanned the air waves.

Time passed without discovery of new information. Her frustration flared when she hit another door closed by Starseeker Command. She paused. "I bet if I were a prince like Garret these doors would open." Denied access to the destination of her parent's mission was frustrating. She decided to post an anonymous request for advice on the Data Stream Advice Board. There must be another place to search for star charts and space mission logs. Answers to questions could be found by topic on the advice board. She entered her question about sources for star charts and ship logs. With any luck, a spacey mega head would send some obscure link.

It still wasn't time to leave for cadet class. Garret would most likely be there. The class of Junior Starseekers had been expecting a visit from Prince Garret. They had been surprised to learn he was going to join their unit after being crowned the king's heir. The Starseeker mission was top priority for Treya. It was logical in a way that he would soon be working with them.

Annie entered Garret's name in a search that led to the royal family tree. The branch of his ancestors led back thousands of years to Nethas, the cradle of all people. From ancient Nethas the royal tree branched out in all directions. Many of these branches ended long before they stretched to the present year of 9010.

Those that did extend that far were labeled by the names of the Seven Realms: Gosar, Nethas, Caldera, Jantar, Sethaly, Taspar and Zebron. The five minor kingdoms were listed among them.

The Gosar branch traced the lineage of the Olsgood kings. It ended with Garret, his brother Gregory and sister Alisa. Clicking on Garret's name brought up a holographic picture of him. It floated in the air before her. His image repeatedly descended a stair and waved to an unseen crowed. *I wonder how uppity and self-centered he is,* she thought while she clicked through pictures of him. *How could anyone avoid having a huge ego with everyone bowing and doing your bidding all your life?*

Annie looked at the other branches of the royal tree. The Nethas branch ended with three children who had all died before she was born. One of the children had a question mark and indicated there might be a child born not long after she was. The rumored missing royalty of Nethas had always seemed odd. *How can you misplace a royal heir?* she scoffed.

AMARIS announced it was time to leave for class. She saved the family tree of royalty for later study.

Annie arrived early to the lecture hall that evening. It was their weekly classroom meeting. She sat near the end of a curving row of seats in front of the holo screen. She pretended to read a book and nervously twirled strands of her hair that she pulled forward to hide her face.

The Junior Starseekers all submitted their weekly assignments from their study stations as they were completed throughout the week. She usually finished hers within a day or two. Most of the others were usually up most of the night before class completing their work.

She noticed Brandon looked preoccupied when he slumped in his usual seat by the door. Annie closed the book on her travel podcom. She slipped it into a pocket and put on a pair of solar-shades. They were standard issue for use during solar cycles in the agriculture domes. She found them useful at times to conceal the abnormal color of her eyes. They also made a good shield against the glares of the other girls in their tailor fitted uniforms. Aunt Constance didn't see the point in buying a uniform just to sit in a classroom once a week. Annie really didn't mind. The standard issue jumpsuit suited her just fine for her daily chores on the station. Melody took her seat next to Annie.

"Are you okay?" Melody asked quietly.

Annie shrugged and replied, "I'm over it—really, I'm fine."

Garret entered the lecture bay with Rick and Curt, his same two friends from sword practice yesterday.

Melody in the next seat nudged her when he first appeared. "He's here!" she gasped in a low whisper.

Annie's gaze locked in on his smiling face. She slid down in her seat and hoped she would go unnoticed.

Garret gave a short speech that she did not hear, stating again the importance of the Starseeker mission. "I hope to become personally acquainted with all of you as we work together on this important mission." His formal speech to the class marked him as a diplomat.

From her seat at the side of the room, she could see his arms stiffen behind his back. *Is he nervous or just excited?* she wondered.

"I'm also looking forward to going on missions to newly discovered worlds that will secure the survival of our people." He then nodded apologetically, "Thank you for allowing me to join your unit and I promise not to bore you with any more speeches." The room echoed with tittering laughter and hushed guffaws.

Annie saw Garret flex his fingers in a nervous manner behind his back. *Perhaps he's more human than I imagined,* she thought.

"This will be a new experience for me. I am usually the only student," Garret smiled sheepishly and headed for a vacant seat in the middle of the room.

Master Jordan formally welcomed him and many stood to receive him. They smiled, clapped and even hooted as Garret took his seat. When reseated the others sat more attentively than usual, with the royal prince sitting among them.

Annie kept her eyes down at her desk. She was determined not to melt down into a childish love struck heap by staring at him. The lights dimmed when Master Jordan began his holoscreen presentation. Annie removed her solar-shades in the low light. Without her shield of darkness Annie still found herself often gazing at Garret.

The lights came back up. Annie repositioned her protective eye-ware. She had no idea what the presentation had been about. While she was secretly gazing again at Garret, he suddenly looked curiously straight at her. Annie's heart skipped a wild beat as she froze for a moment without breathing. She hoped the sudden warmth in her cheeks was not visible.

"Ah! I see young Brandon has managed to escape again. I'm afraid he finds working on star shuttles more interesting than my lectures."

The Starseeker students laughed.

"Since Prince Garret will not be appointed as an officer until later this evening. He will be dinning today with the cadet officers in training. If you have any questions you would like to ask him this would be your opportunity. Class dismissed," Master Jordan announced and released them to the food court for dinner. Annie was the first one out of the door.

Annie first dropped by the shuttle bay to ask if Brandon would join them for dinner. But Tad said he never showed up. *Where else could Brandon have run off too?* she wondered to herself.

When she arrived at the food court, all of the Junior Starseekers were gathered around Garret's table.

There was standing room only by then, so Annie sat at a small table off to the side. She checked her wristband for what was on her duty itinerary for the next day.

"I think I've met all of you now," Prince Garret said, "except for the girl wearing solar-shades," he said, nodding in Annie's direction.

"Oh, that's just Jumpsuit Annie," Celia said in an annoying high titter. "She always has her nose in a book."

Melody frowned at her remark and left the group to sit with Annie. "Celia is telling Garret you always have your nose in a book. At least we don't always have our noses in the air looking down on others."

Annie laughed. Melody had often proved to be a loyal friend and source of comfort through their four years of training. Melody then yelped in surprise, "It's Brandon!" She pointed over Annie's shoulder.

Across the food court and behind a counter she saw Brandon flipping zorker burgers. Annie followed Melody after she dashed over to the zork and seafood counter.

"Can't a guy earn an honest quadmar without people thinking you're strange?" Brandon explained that he had been caught speeding one too many times and he needed the cash for graduation. "Did you know that those automated traffic zones record and add up points for every little thing you do wrong when you're flying? Then they can automatically drain every last quadmar out of your credit account and put you on probation for months at a time."

"I think I've heard something about that," Annie answered. She and Melody both grinned.

"Don't laugh! My dad was so mad that he told me I had to get a job to earn back what the zone guards took." Brandon was then pulled away to serve a customer with the head chef giving him the evil eye.

Annie and Melody both laughed and shook their heads when they walked away.

"I really do hope he learns to fly better after this," Melody confided. "Have you ever flown with him when he says, *'We're hauling buuuuuns?'*"

"Yeah, once!" Annie said. "Pretty scary!" She smiled and then looked down. There was something she wanted to tell Melody but she wasn't sure if she should.

Melody noticed the change in her. "Is there something wrong?" she asked.

"No, there's nothing *wrong*." Annie paused trying to think of how to explain. "It's just that—well, today is my sixteenth birthday and Aunt Constance is spending the week in Caldera. Not that she ever . . . ."

"Your sixteenth birthday!" Melody exploded. "Why didn't you tell me earlier? We could have done something, gone somewhere. My mom would have baked you a cake."

"No," Annie said. "I wouldn't have wanted you to go to the trouble. Really!"

Melody slumped with a dejected look on her face.

Something suddenly caught her eye. "Well, the least you can do is let me buy you some frozen sorba." She took Annie's hand and pulled her to the food counter.

"Melody, this really isn't necessary. I'm almost sorry I mentioned it now."

"You love sorba. There is no point in denying it."

Annie grinned and gave in. Melody knew her weakness when it came to food not in their training diet. "Thanks Melody!" she said and dug in to the melting cream with a spoon. "You really shouldn't have, but it tastes great." They were both rolling their eyes with their mouths full of the delectable frozen treat. "Hmmm! That is so good!" Annie crooned. They were so wrapped up in ecstasy they hadn't noticed anything else around them.

There was a small contingent of Junior Starseekers still hanging behind with Garret. He seemed to be making his way towards the shuttle bay exit, but were stopped short when they encountered the two girls in their revelry. Celia was almost glued to Garret's side.

"Aw, would you look at that!" Celia scolded, in her pinched annoying voice. "Flagrant violations of dietary parameters for cadets in training—and in front of the Prince himself, no less."

"Today just happens to be Annie's birthday," Melody responded in a superior tone. "We are allowed to celebrate on special occasions." Annie's jaw stiffened. She had lost her appetite.

"Is that sorba?" Garret asked. "I hear it's

delicious. I'll have to try it sometime."

Annie's eyes rose back up to meet Garret's through her solar-shades. She held him suspect in her gaze. *Surely the prince of Gosar eats sorba all the time.* Garret was clearly not taking Celia's side in following regulations. The sudden look of dejection on Celia's face was irresistibly gratifying. One corner of Annie's mouth curled up.

Before Celia could make another remark, Garret gave them all a short formal bow. "Thank you all for your friendly welcome, but I must return to my duties at the palace." He took a quick glance in Annie's direction before he smiled and turned away.

Annie's breath caught and she had to remind herself to keep breathing. Celia gave Annie a glare before she and the others broke off to return to their Starseeker duties.

Annie thanked Melody again for the special treat and declined an unexpected invitation to a family dinner. She enjoyed spending time with Melody's parents, but it always made the aching of the hollow space inside grow more intense. She was simply glad that Melody had cared enough to ask.

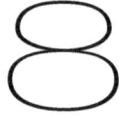

SHUTTLE RACE
DAY 3

ANNIE CLUNG TO THE RAIL overlooking the spinning gravity geode in the center of the station's hollow mid section. A sharp pang of agony ran up her spine to join the guilt of involving others in unauthorized racing hung on her shoulders. She could see it everywhere, bright flamboyant color shouting for attention on walkways of every deck.

Oh no, this isn't good, Annie groaned to herself. *Will Uncle Jordan ever forgive me?*

Graduating cadets had taken to wearing garish colors when off-duty. Since they were not allowed to leave the space station, it signaled to others to "Leave me alone." The growing popularity of *Flamware* added to a charge of anticipation in the air. The final days of training were coming to an end.

I hope officers don't wonder why so many cadets are off

duty, Annie thought as she rehashed the many things that could go wrong.

Her favorite lavender scarf seemed pale compared to the multicolored sea of cadets that flowed by. Orders to stop this practice were expected any day, but so far they had not been issued. A tall fellow wearing a rainbow colored shirt slipped one of the many notes that had been passed among her classmates the last few days. She checked to make sure she was out of security cam range before she read it.

```
Stow equipment for 3 escape
routes by 24:00. Flight crews
only at 01:00 Launch. All
others to monitor on flight
training band - Password
ZORKER - Destroy this message
to avoid hands of Command.
```

19:00 glowed on Annie's wristband. She ran to the trans-tube next to the stairs and pressed one of its glowing blue buttons. The floors sped by as it carried her down through the station. She sprang through the door when it opened and headed for the large shuttle bay doors. She was in with a scan of her hand and was eagerly looking about when she spied two pairs of legs under the T35 shuttle with the hopped up engines.

Brandon was in a heated debate. "The higher compression won't blow out the heat baffles because of the increased angle of the jet valves, I swear."

"But the engineering diagnostics don't agree." Melody fumed in frustration.

"Like I said for the hundredth time. Engineering schematics don't allow for this kind of adjustment."

Annie kicked at both of their feet. "We are way beyond time for this, you two. Engineering all aircraft was scheduled for completion weeks ago." Her officer training had kicked in and she was determined to bring discipline to her crew.

"We were just trying to fix the flicker in Brandon's new cloaking device." Melody said from under the spaceship. "Then Brandon started playing with the jet valves."

Brandon and Melody rolled out from under the shuttle. Their appearance made Annie's jaw drop. Brandon's black shirt was a blazing display of blinking colored lights. A spaceship holovision dove and swooped about. It cleverly appeared to fly out of the shirt and dive back in another direction. Melody's white cap was even more eye catching. Shooting stars of colored light shot out of a sparkling white mist that crowned her head.

"Hi guys!?" Annie stuttered in shock. "Uh, don't you think that might attract too much attention? I mean maybe we shouldn't be advertising so many of us are off-duty right now."

"Are you crazy?" Brandon gloated, having been rewarded by her awe struck face. He was the chief instigator of the new flaming *off-duty* ware. "Our last year is almost over. They would think something was up if we weren't wearing strange stuff. Besides lots of trainees are often off-duty at the same time when they return from training missions—we've been over this." Brandon frowned and his grumpy face had become super serious above the playful joyride on his shirt.

Annie was full of pleading concern. "I'm serious," Annie retorted but couldn't hold back her laugher as she swiped her hand through the sparkling holovision diving about on his shirt. She shook her head and relented to her friend. "Please Brandon, Command could order us all confined to our quarters for disrupting ship operations if we rock the boat too soon. We could all be seriously in for it, as it is."

Brandon half grinned seeing Annie's struggle. "Fine," he relented and killed the flashing lights. "No colored warning lights flashing in their faces."

Melody sighed and turned off the shooting light display on her hat. "And no more fireworks until they really start," she relented.

Annie cringed in agony over the disciplinary action she knew would come for them all if security discovered their race.

"Are you getting nervous, Ann?" Brandon gave her a reassuring pat on the shoulder. "No backing out now, little sister. It's time to shoot this show off in to space." His excitement beamed out of every pore.

Annie could hardly believe their mad scheme was

about to come true. They had been staging this last championship race before graduation for years now, but doubt still plagued her. Senior rescue and medical squads had been positioned, but so many things could still go wrong.

"Seriously," Brandon soothed her, "flight clearance, security cams—it's all been covered by our whiz-kid here." Without thinking, his arm looped around Melody in a hug. His face then turned bright red and he awkwardly smiled while he removed his arm her shoulders.

Annie and Melody both glanced at each other with a grin. Brandon was never embarrassed about anything except when it came to Melody.

"Well—uh—," he stammered. "We better get some rack time in before the race."

"Meet back here at 00:50 for launch," Annie said and put out her fist.

"To another win for the Phantom Firestar," Melody said, and she also put out her fist.

Brandon's fist reached out to join theirs. "And may we fly like the ancient Firestar." Brandon said, and they all punched upward and shouted "Who-rah!"

Cadets had turned in early to sleep bays to nap before the late night race. Annie's study pod blinked to life when she entered her sleep bay.

"Pod off," she directed and the study pod station shut down. Her droid projected a game board. "Not tonight E-Chip." The droid bleeped several times and shut down.

She passed her study station and pressing a button on the wall to open a drawer. She laid her jacket and jumpsuit in the drawer and it retracted back into the wall. Turning to face her bed rack, she touched her forehead, kissed her fingers and transferred it with a touch to the carved plaque of a flaming tree over her bed for good luck. The light in the room faded when she rolled onto the recessed bed. The blue foam mattress molded around her as she pulled the blanket up.

Annie pulled a small book from a niche above her head. Few people used or even owned antiquated books, but Annie found them comforting. She skimmed over the familiar legend of the ancient Firestar ship. It told how the orb from its core had made it possible for the first people to live on Treya. It was now in an amplifying harness at the weather control center in Omara. The firestar orb was a mysterious natural mineral formation not found on Treya and Engineers had found it impossible to duplicate. When growing-up, she had always wondered how it had turned an icy world into green fertile fields. If the legend was true, couldn't it happen again?

She closed the worn leather book and returned it to its recessed compartment. "Lights off!" She sighed as she thought about the day. Her last thoughts were always of her parents and also now of Garret. Their faces floated through her thoughts before she drifted off to sleep.

Garret slashed and warded off Rick's blows with a practice light sword. He suddenly stopped in frustration and turned off his sword. "I don't get why I have to be a great swordsman." He reached to his side, "All I have to do is pull my laser gun and you're toast." He pretended to fire at Rick.

Rick smiled, "What if you don't have your gun?" With a flick of his sword Garret's gun went flying and the tip of his sword glowed brightly under Garret's chin.

Garret's stunned brow rose, "I see your point." His nervous respect for Rick's weapon came out in a laugh and he smiled.

"Enough of this charade!" Curt broke in. "We need to get to the shuttle bay if we're going to be in this unauthorized race tonight."

Garret had finally persuaded Curt and Rick to let him enter the final shuttle race. Curt had been monitoring the races for the last year. The time and location of the shuttle races were always different. Practice simulation runs had always been made available by the unknown race organizers. Despite their trainee status, pilots would be well rehearsed for a competitive race.

They each put on a helmet with a dark visor before leaving battle practice. Garret was eager to test himself in a competition where his identity could remain a mystery.

A black helmet with a black sun shield hid Annie's face while she stood before the cadets who had assembled in the launch bay hangar. Melody and Brandon stood on either side in matching gear with Phantom Firestar blazed on the shoulder. The ancient Firestar had brought their people to this planet. Its namesake had brought Annie's crew to the final race as the champions to be beaten. Her anticipation was making her jittery and she struggled to compose herself.

"All twelve crews are present," Melody reported. An unfamiliar team dressed in dark blue stood among them. Skyhawk was written on their flight suits.

"The time to launch has come, whether you are prepared or not." Annie's helmet made her voice unrecognizable in the low bass voice of a man. Anonymity made the competition more unbiased and fair while also protecting the identity of others if caught.

Brandon and Melody handed out track and

targeting guide chips for pilots to load into their ship navigation.

"This will guide you to the starting lineup," Annie continued. "It will countdown automatically to start the race and will not wait if you are late. Our destination, if you weren't able to guess, is the asteroid belt of the Derius Moon. Like the simulator, the fastest and safest routes through the moving asteroids will be calculated to guide you. It is strongly suggested that you do not deviate off course for everyone's safety. Like before, there are emergency squads stationed along the course."

"Your pilot, navigator and engineer, will all participate in target shooting." Annie moved to the back end of her ship, and placed her hand on a target. "Floating targets like this will appear like they did in simulation. They will register shots from your ship on your tracking chip. Shots registered on the rear burn flaps of other shuttles earn bonus points. These can make up for missed targets. Even if you fly a fast race you must also have a high shooting score to win."

Annie turned to a cadet holding a recording camcom. "This broadcast will begin again at the start of the race. Shut off the cam." What followed was for the flight crews only.

"Until now," Annie spoke loud with authority, "the course hazards around stationary objects in our practice live races have been predictable. For the final live race it was decided that moving obstacles would provide a higher challenge. The real risk and danger for you is much greater and no one here wants to end up like Captain Toren killed in the last obstacle course run by Starseekers four years ago." Heads turned and feet shifted among the group in the pause that followed. "If your pilot did not score consistent perfect runs in simulation or did not get in the required real flight time—. I strongly urge you not to meet at the Derius Moon." A murmur spread through the group.

"There will be no shame if your crew does not start, or pulls out of the race." The deep voice from the speaker in Annie's helmet rang out through the hangar. "We are all unknown here. I urge you before you decide, to consider the safety of your crewmates as you would on a real mission."

The tension in the air was uncomfortable until Annie's head rose from thought. My hope is that your navigation skill will continue to improve when you rerun this course in simulation. May the creator of the ancient Firestar guide you safely across the finish line. That is all." The crews headed for their ships. Many of them were more hesitant than usual while others dashed off to their ships.

"Do you really think some of them won't show?" Melody asked when they boarded their ship.

Annie shrugged before she climbed into the cockpit. "I don't know. I only know that unless some of them have improved, they really shouldn't."

"Heck no!" Brandon said. "They're all too cocky. They all have to be a bunch of arrogant hot shots to even sign up for this stuff."

Annie turned to Brandon. "Is that what you think I am?"

Brandon's hands came up. "Oh no, I didn't mean you—it's not like all pilots are competitive jerks. Uh—you're different—you started learning to fly before you were six. You—you . . . ."

"Oh stop," Annie cut him off. "I just hope those who should, will reconsider. Flying fast is dangerous. You know, it's that tunnel vision thing that Master Jordan talks about. Your mind closes off and you don't always see what's coming."

The launch bay doors open and the trio quickly buckled themselves in for departure. Starlight glinted off the tuwesian skin of the T35 Phantom Firestar and shimmered on the shield beyond the atmospheric barrier. Melody uploaded tracking to navigation and both Annie and Brandon gave the thumbs up for the internal systems that were a go for ignition. A tremor from the engine core grew as the control panel lit up and the wings flickered in a shifting displacement of time.

"Phantom, you are go for launch," Brandon's voice crackled in Annie's headset. The shuddering ship rumbled in the confined space, ready for release.

Annie said a quick prayer before giving the command to, "Launch!"

Melody depressed the red thruster control and the T35 shot past the launch bay doors into the vast darkness of space with a tremendous thrust throwing them back in their seats.

"Wahoo-oo-oo!" Brandon called out despite the vibrating force stretching his face. "La-unch is-izz the coo-ool-est th-ing ever-er-er-r-r-r!"

As the gravitational force was left behind, the feeling of weightlessness took over and released the press of their bodies into their seats. Simulated launches without G-force were nothing like this. A slow moving sea of clouds passed beneath them. The enormous planet of Treya made Annie feel like a floating speck of dust.

"Planned course to rendezvous is laid in," Melody confirmed while tapping the control screen.

"Practice flight, proceed at mock three to jump point," Annie ordered.

On the rear view screen, the Starseeker Station quickly shrank into nothingness above a planet destined soon to be lonely and lifeless. Melody reported, "Three crews failed to launch from the station.

"They can always claim mechanical failure," Annie suggested. Flipping her headset back to flight command she ordered, "Initiate warp one as we enter the jump zone." When the flight group shot forward, a few shuttles blasted ahead as if there was a race to the starting line. Annie hung back with the main group.

There was no point in speeding; they couldn't start until the countdown.

A stray wrench floated up beside Annie. "I see someone's been untidy. Brandon, stow the wrench and anything else you left lying about."

Brandon quickly floated over to snag the wrench when he caught sight of something off to the left. "Hey guys! Take a look at the new T36."

Melody leaned over for a better view. "I hear they're really fast. I bet it's that new Skyhawk crew."

Brandon dismissed her worries with a confident shrug. "It may be a fast assembly job. But, our custom modified jets have it where it counts." He flipped around and floated back to buckle into the gunnery.

Annie looked the new shuttle over. "Just the same—I hope they aren't any good at target shooting." Annie worried to herself, *Brandon and Melody are both good shots but some of the others are better.*

"No time for worry now, Gambler's Alley straight ahead," Melody reported. "Keep your eyes peeled for fast moving strays." A floating swarm of asteroids stretched out before them.

Brandon's chair rose into the gunnery position behind Annie. "Targeting Tracker engaged," he reported.

"1:15 and counting," Melody said. She brought up the transparent targeting screen before her chair also rose into position.

"Hey guys," Brandon said. "There's only eight

ships at the starting line."

Annie's rhythmic sweep of the control panels paused. "Someone must have turned back." The danger in earlier unauthorized races had been in the number of ships. Now only the top competitors were left to risk being caught by Starseeker command. Thruster gauges rose as the final micropecs ticked away—five, four, three, two, one. The red starting light flooded the cockpit.

"Launch!" Brandon shouted.

Annie punched both red buttons on the two handles of the steering column in her grip. Their ship shot forward and the inertia pressed them back into their seats.

The T36 was fast and edged ahead taking the lead.

"Target right," Melody called as she and Brandon started firing.

"I got a burn flap on the T36!" Brandon cried out.

"Targets, Brandon!" Annie ordered "Don't forget the high points on primary targets!"

The very first turn around an asteroid caught the T36 Skyhawk swinging wide before Annie brought the Phantom in to cut a tight corner and to pull ahead. The course carried the racing ships deeper into the asteroid belt. Colored flight lines popped into Annie's view. The red line was the safest course while blue lines offered alternate courses. Melody and Brandon continued to call out targets and to fire guns. Simulated explosions lit the course confirming a flurry of laser beam contacts with targets.

Annie saw a ship tumbled to the right. Another ship followed in a controlled spin and they both flew off to open space. *He hit something hard, but he's in one piece.*

"Down to six ships," Melody called out. Blue and red lights on a rescue shuttle flashed by.

Annie fought to maintain the ship on the course guides, as she caught herself flying too wide in a turn. *Hold it together,* she told herself. *Rescue will be back at the station before you will.* Two ships flying tight in the turn past her by. She knew she had to calm herself and focus. *Safe and tight.* She told herself.

The Skyhawk pulled further ahead in a series of straight-aways with shallow turns. Their target hits scored one after another and their rank increased rapidly on the game screen.

Pulsing blue lasers streaked out from the ships causing sprays of exploding light to burst in the path of those who followed as they dodged through the shifting asteroids growing in number. The score of the Phantom followed close behind the leader. Annie made two tight turns and pulled ahead of the second ship. She found a rhythm in the curving path and was soon right behind the T36, after it faltered in the sharper turns. Annie saw her chance, and with two tight turns, she pulled back into the lead.

Brandon's gun paused. "Aw, I missed again. Can't you fly any straighter?" Annie heard Brandon, but she blocked out his complaint and he returned to his gunfire. *The end is coming. We can still lose it in the straightaway if I don't build a lead in the turns or stay on course.*

"The T36 took it wide," Brandon called out. "The Skyhawk is falling away."

Annie rounded the last bend out of the asteroid belt and punched the thrusters into the final straightaway. Victory was theirs as they headed for the last glowing beacon with their goal outlined in lights.

"YES! The Phantom Firestar will win it again as the sure favorite of her adoring fans." Brandon crooned is his announcers voice.

"Uh oh," Melody called out. "I hate to say this but, the Skyhawk is gaining fast."

"Eyes front, Mel," Annie ordered. "Watch for targets!"

The finish line grew closer. *I'm sure we gained a big enough lead in the turns.* But, she saw it from the corner of her eye. A glimmering shadow that not only threatened to take the victory from them, but seemed destined to do so. The sleek gleaming nose of the Skyhawk crept smoothly forward inch-by-inch with a hyper dual rockets drawing up beside them. Desperation raced through Annie's mind. *Only a few micro tarns left. Stay focused and hold it straight.* They were almost nose-to-nose—The finish line flashed by.

The rapid heartbeat in Annie's chest slowed and the whine of the engine core died into a silent glide.

Time seemed suspended as they waited for the announcement of the winner on their headsets. "The T36 Skyhawk regained lost space in the straight-away," the announcer shouted, "but was nosed out by the T35 Phantom who has hung on for the win."

"Whoa-hoo-oo-oo!!!" they all shouted. The exhilaration of the win coursed through Annie. The shear elation was like none she had ever felt before.

The announcer's words also filled Annie with relief. They had done it! A shiver ran up her spin when she realized that against all odds they had edged out the fastest ship flying. Brandon and Melody's hopped up engines had held their own. Annie flipped the ship in a double loop. There was still the target shooting to factor in to claim a real win. So, they swung back to the finish zone to wait for the final tallies.

"Only three contenders finished the treacherous run through Gambler's Alley," The race monitor continued to report while the tallies were calculated and confirmed.

"Three other ships must have pulled out during the race," Melody summed up.

"Rescue squads report one casualty," the monitor reported and paused.

Annie's breath caught and her heart pounded in her ears.

"The first ship knocked off the course suffered surface damage to the ship, but none were seriously injured on board."

Annie sighed with relief. It was all over. She hadn't realized what a huge relief it would be when the run was safely complete.

The standings flashed on the forward screen. The T36 was in first place and had won. *How can that be?* Both of the other ships had higher shooting scores. They had only managed to hold onto second place because the third ship had fallen so far behind.

Annie saw Melody and Brandon's disappointment. "So they got some lucky shots in, we're still winners as I see it."

"Good," Melody said, "because I am not flying on that course again."

Brandon nodded with wide eyes. "That was sure some crazy ride."

Annie smiled and nodded in agreement. "Let's get back to base before we're missed."

The returning shuttles flew in a V formation with the T36 at point. It was the last race of their training days. Though none of them were in a rush for it to end, they also didn't want to be caught. Every minipec counted as shuttles streaked back to the space station. They were sure to lose their positions as officers on Starseeker missions if command caught wind of their race.

On the flight back to the Seeker station Annie's regret at having staged this event returned. Her old game with Brandon to improve their flight skills was no longer a game. The deception required to fly the races in actual ships had put the careers of many at risk.

When the ships neared the station the red alert was sent by the lookouts. Ship security had somehow been alerted and would soon be in launch bay. The T36 and two other ships, peeled off and headed for the planet's surface. The Phantom crew removed their flight suits to uncover the maintenance bay jumpsuits they were wearing.

Brandon stashed the flight suits in the cargo hold.

Annie smoothly landed the T35 in the shuttle bay. In a few micropecs they had the ship locked down and were quickly out the shuttle bay door.

Please don't let anyone get caught, Annie prayed while the crews slipped out through back stairwells and service accesses. *Security will find no one in flight suits. All aircraft will be locked down and thanks to Mel, the security cams will show nothing. Tad's off on break and can deny seeing anything. The plan is flawless. Nothing can go wrong.* But that was just it, anything could go wrong.

INTERROGATION

DAY 4

THERE WAS CONFUSION AND GOSSIP the next morning when all cadets in training were questioned by Starseeker security. Some cadets reported odd questions were asked that had nothing to do with unauthorized racing.

Annie sat at a table with a man dressed in black on the other side. A security guard stood by the door.

"So, you say you spent some hours in practice flight training last night."

"Yes, sir, I already answered all these questions."

"Yes, but though you claim responsibility for this incident you refuse to name the others who were with you."

Annie knew their purpose was to find someone to blame and they wouldn't stop until they did. The line of questions then took an unexpected turn.

"You are the daughter of Commander Bryan Roeshell and his wife Ellen."

"Yes."

"You appear to be wearing contact lenses."

"Yes."

"Will you remove them please?"

"Why?"

"Is there a problem?"

"No."

"Then remove them now, please."

Annie had no idea what these questions had to do with flying an obstacle course. The reports of unusual questions had been true. She removed her contacts with a feeling she had been cornered.

"Your eyes have an unusual color. Why do you cover them?"

Annie could feel herself getting angry. These were personal questions that had nothing to do with her conduct on the ship. "Why should it matter or be any of your business?"

"In-deed! When you were six you lost your parents, and lived with your Aunt Constance. She was your father's sister?" The interrogator seemed to notice her growing hostility, but remained cold and direct.

"Yes. But, why should that matter?"

"Do you have any other living relatives that you are aware of?"

"Maybe, but why should I tell you? You already

seem to know everything."

"Just answer the question."

"No, I'm not telling you anything unless you tell me why?"

"Very well, Miss. I think we have all we need to know."

The man stood and turned to the guard. "You may tell the commander I am done for the day," he said and left the room.

The guard looked surprised at Annie. "I guess you're free to go." He left the room leaving the door open for her.

What was all that about? Annie wondered. *I was the last person he wanted to question even though there were others waiting. Somehow they knew I was involved. How many others will the inquisitor accuse? Would they all be sent home to their families humiliated? I'll never be allowed to become a Starseeker now.* A terrifying thought slammed into her chest. *I'll never be able to search for my parents. The anguish drove into the pit of her stomach. How could she not have seen this outcome?* There was nothing she could do now except wait for charges to be made by Starseeker command and security guards to come arrest her and the others. *Everything I've done my whole life has been for nothing.*

Annie put her contacts back in with a shaky hand and left to return to her scheduled duty.

Later that day, Annie stood alone before Starseeker Admiral Dakar and his aide after a messenger had come with orders for her to report.

"This is Annie, Sir," the aide reported.

The Admiral dismissed his aide and he gazed at her as he considered his words. Annie hung her head low. She had never foreseen this truly happening. "Annie, it would seem from the Inquisitor's report and statements from your fellow cadets that you have instigated a whole lot of trouble for yourself and others. What is your last name?"

"Roeshell, Sir."

"Roeshell—you wouldn't be the daughter of Bryan Roeshell would you?"

"Yes, sir."

"Bryan was a very good pilot. He also had a way of getting into trouble. It is stated here in this report, that you and your crew instigated a series of unauthorized races. Is this true?"

"Yes, sir."

"But, how can that be when all the others have only reported rumors that the leader was a young man? Can you explain?"

"Yes, sir, we kept our identity secret from the others. I used a voice modifier in my helmet. I sounded like a man."

"So it's true, that none of you really knew who they raced against?"

"Yes, sir."

"Who made this voice modifier for you to use?"

"I did, Sir," Annie confessed. Melody had

installed the voice modifier, but there was no reason to destroy anyone else's future.

"I see—you and your friends have all refused to give the names of the other conspirators. This would be highly commended, had you been caught by an enemy in an act of war. But, this involves students in training for scientific research. The only reason we have you here I understand is because you wanted to take responsibility for the actions of everyone involved. Is that true?"

"Yes, sir, I was the one who led and directed the others."

"You want me to have you punished and no one else. By saying you are responsible for everything, makes your statement unreliable and any claim of guilt suspect. But what testimony is there to verify you were the leader? There is none."

The doors to the chamber opened. Prince Garret and Master Jordan marched forward.

"What is this? This is a closed meeting. I won't tolera—"

"Pardon me Sir," Prince Garret said and gave a sharp nod. "I would like to testify on behalf of the accused."

"Testify?" Admiral Deker bowed at the waist in reply. "Pardon me, Your Highness, but what could you have possibly witnessed?"

"I was at the race, Sir."

"You were?" Annie asked in honest surprise.

"In what capacity were you present, Your Highness?" The Admiral asked while he struggled to maintain control of the proceeding.

"I won the race," Garret simply stated.

"You? That was you?" Annie stared at him in disbelief.

Admiral Deker was quite aware that the Prince's claim was a total surprise to Annie. "I see, and the person claiming to be the leader of this whole affair had no idea that the winner of the competition was the royal prince of Gosar." The Admiral shook his head and returned to his chair. "This is all highly irregular."

"If I may, Admiral?"

"Yes, Master Jordan. Is there something you would like to add?" Admiral Deker frowned in agitation.

"I would simply like to say that these obstacle runs were performed under the safest conditions possible."

"You call racing through an asteroid belt safe?"

"No, not usually—I would admit that the final course did surpass training standards. But, I understand from Prince Garret that participants trained for many hours in simulation and were required to have a thousand tarens of real flight time before the competition. They were also told that if their pilot had not scored consistent perfect runs in simulation that they should not race."

Admiral Deker's frown had softened. "Is this

what you heard Prince Garret?"

"Yes Admiral, that is what the leader—who I thought was a boy at the time—said. He, or *she*, also emphasized the great danger we were putting ourselves and our crew into and that we should consider the risk, as we would for any mission."

"Did you, Prince Garret, consider the dangers you, as a future leader of your people, were putting yourself into?"

"Yes, sir. I take that responsibility very seriously. I felt I was prepared."

"And you won—because of this simulator training."

"We were also provided with a guidance program that calculated the safest routes through the asteroid field."

Admiral Deker peered curiously at Annie. "And where did this guidance program come from? Did you create this program, Annie?"

"Yes, Sir."

The Admiral paused in thought. "Regulations forbid competitive racing because it often forces people into conditions they are unprepared for. The need to avoid the shame of failure would take priority over good judgment."

Garret wasted no time in offering defense to take advantage of his thoughtful mood. "Annie also emphasized that there would be no shame if we decided not to run the course, or even pull out after it began."

"Because no one knew the identity of the others." The Admiral finished. "Did anyone pull out of the race?"

"Three crews did not leave the Space Station, Sir," Annie submitted.

Garret added, "A forth turned back before the start and four pulled out during the course. Only three pilots finished the race."

"That makes eleven crews involved."

"There were twelve, sir. One did spin out early in the course with minor damage to the ship," Annie admitted.

"That was very fortunate. I know there were emergency squads. They were the only ones we could identify. Master Jordan, your authorization was given for the release of the shuttles for practice flight."

"I am aware that my authorization code was used to approve the training flights."

"I see. So, you will not deny that you submitted the code."

Jordan paused before speaking. "Cadets are subject to danger daily here in space. But, I admit that I was aware that obstacle courses were being run— nothing was taken—and funds were provided by the participants. But I did not stop their activity. So, you see if anyone is to blame it is I."

"You have put me in a most difficult position, Master Jordan. To expose this would jeopardize the entire Starseeker program. Can you imagine the scandal with Prince Garret and an instructor of the Starseeker forces being involved?" Admiral Deker was beside himself. "I can see I have only one real option."

The Admiral returned to his desk and turned to address them. "The participation of cadets in competitive obstacle runs is hereby authorized by Starseeker Command. They will from this day forward take place only with the full knowledge of Command. Is that clear, Miss Roeshell?"

"Yes, Sir." The shock of the quick turn of events caught her by surprise.

"This matter is officially closed. All records of this proceeding are to be sealed. You are all dismissed."

When they heard this, Annie and Garret gaped at each other with wide-eyed relief and laughed at each other's expression.

Master Jordan put his hands on their shoulders and turned them around to leave.

"Oh, Miss Roeshell." The Admiral's words stopped Annie, causing her to turn back, her relief gone. "I would like to speak to you later about this program for navigating asteroid fields."

"Oh, yes sir!" Annie bowed in penitent relief. If the survival of the people was not in the Starseekers hands, and Prince Garret had not been involved, she would not have escaped punishment. Gratefully, she turned and left. Escape from judgement removed the worries from her mind and she oddly felt light and carefree.

Curt and Rick met Garret outside command.

"Do we have to go now?" Garret asked.

"There are only four days left before your crowning as the Gosar heir, Your Highness. The palace has many details to work out."

Garret turned to Annie and Master Jordan. "It seems the rest of my day has been planned for me as usual." Garret sighed and seemed reluctant to go.

"You will be back tomorrow for command training with the cadets, Your Highness."

"Yes, I'll look forward to that." Garret gave a short nod. "Good day to you both, Master Jordan and Miss Roeshell." He lingered, only a moment, before he left with his friends trailing behind him.

Annie looked sheepishly at Master Jordan. "Thank you for coming to rescue me. I'm glad for Garret's sake this mess with racing all worked out."

"Yes," Uncle Jordan agreed, "we are very lucky that this *mess* is all cleaned up and behind us."

Annie then remembered the Inquisitor. "Did you hear about some of the odd questions being asked—the ones about family connections? He also asked about the color of my eyes."

Master Jordan took her arm and started to walk with her. "I heard some reports. It was probably a loyalty tactic to help force out the truth."

This sounded like an excuse but she could tell the questions bothered Master Jordan.

"I think it would be best if the leader of unauthorized racing stayed in her room the rest of the day."

Annie frowned, but knew the punishment was far less than she deserved. They parted near her squad bay and she texted a message to Melody about the Admiral's decision.

Word that command had authorized future competitive flights spread like wild fire through the ship. Victory fanned the flames of celebration among the cadets in their final days of training.

Annie stopped among groups of others who had gathered to look over the mid-ship deck rails. Racing ships with blasting lasers dodging through asteroids in gambler's alley, flashed by on the huge central holoscreen. Someone had overridden the ships information board to broadcast the race. She smiled until she remembered the discipline she narrowly escaped. *I probably would not be a cadet right now if Garret hadn't saved me. He is the only reason I still have a chance to find my parents.* She pictured his friendly face in her mind and warmth flushed her cheeks.

10

FIELD EXERCISE

ANNIE'S TEETH CLENCHED as Brandon flew the speeding shuttle low into the test site. A slight tremor ran along the floor boards until they were caught in a cushion of air and settled into the snow.

An expedition unit of cadets lined both sides of the cargo transport. Annie wondered what sort of test Uncle Jordan had prepared for them.

Garret took the command position and stood facing the forward flight crew. At age eighteen, he appeared to stand tall and confident but the edge of tension in his movements said otherwise. He had only recently joined the Junior Starseekers.

"Navigator report," he ordered.

"Atmosphere is non-lethal, sir," Brandon reported with a strong note of sarcasm.

Garret turned to the mission crew with a smile

that looked relaxed. "The atmosphere on Treya is non-lethal," he reported in obvious humor. "This exercise will be performed without helmets and oxygen. Full thermal gear is to be worn at all times. Stay with your squads and remember this is not a competition. As on a real mission, landing parties are to work together for the safety of all." His eyes at the end rested briefly on Annie. Her breath caught and she looked away. His safety instruction reminded her of how he defending her actions to Admiral Deker.

"Thank you, Prince Garret," Master Jordan said when he bowed and came to stand beside him. "Cadets, you have your objective and data scanners. Let's go find what possible life could exist in the frigid regions of northern Treya." He turned to Garret, "I'll remain here while you lead the mission. You may dismiss the Company"

"Company Dismissed!" Garret ordered. The young Starseekers turned and grinned to each other. This was Garret's first command and he seemed a bit nervous.

Melody smiled and whispered to Annie, "I hope this doesn't take long. I hate cold weather."

"All the more reason to work fast as a unit," Annie said with a wink, and strapped on her backpack. Today Annie felt older than her fifteen years. Somehow the critical importance of responsibilities that would soon be hers weighed heavy on her mind. The young Starseekers pulled on hoods, gloves, headsets and snow goggles before they left the shuttle. Garret sent squads in different directions from the base of the shuttle ramp. An icy blast of wind pelted them with tiny ice crystals when they trudged off into the drifting snow.

Annie, Melody and Brandon found high ground and started scanning for life signs. Annie's headset remained silent. *No one is picking up anything or my headcom is dead.* After they trudged up a higher ridge, Annie decided to run alternate scan combinations. She scanned the ridge before them for heat on Subterranean Thermal and recorded a faint response.

"I got something!" Annie announced on her headset. "Squad five has made contact with Sub-thermal." The rest of the unit all switched over their scanners and started moving up the high ridge. Annie and her squad were the first to top the ridge. Below them was a pool of aqua blue water in a valley of snow. Wisps of vapor rose from the heated water and it had a strange blue glow.

"I'm getting low level life readings from that pond," Melody said.

"Let's see what it is," Brandon said and he took off, bounding down the hillside.

"Brandon, No!" Annie yelled after him. "We're supposed to scan the surface beneath the snow!" She rolled her eyes and muttered in disgust before she followed. "He's like a starving horse with blinders on. He can see the carrot but not the chuck holes." The rest of the unit topped the far end of the ridge in time to see Brandon charging across the bottom of the small valley toward the misty pond. Suddenly, Brandon dropped into the snow up to his arm pits.

"Whoa!" Melody's worried eyes turned to Annie, "Are chuck holes that big?"

"Brandon!" Annie yelled, "Don't move!" She turned to Melody, "follow in his footsteps and scan for holes in the rock." Quickly they made their way down near Brandon. Annie scanned Brandon's position. She could see Melody's fear when her expression turned to panic. They knew the fatally unexpected dangers Starseekers faced daily and Mel's constant worries about Brandon were no help at this point.

"The scan shows he's in a slush pit no deeper than his chest."

"I'm stuck!"

"You certainly are!" Annie hooted and laughed.

"The good news is you won't sink any farther." Melody's mixed emotions played on her face. She tried to sound encouraging when she half smiled, but worry creased her brow.

"Well, I'm glad you're both enjoying this. A little help, please!"

Annie pulled a rope out of Melody's backpack and turned back to Brandon. "Raise your hands and catch the rope." She swung one end out to him. The first toss was short but the second toss landed within reach. Brandon looped and tied the rope around his chest.

"Got it! You can pull now. I hope you girls are stronger than you look." Brandon's teeth were now chattering. Annie lifted the rope and Melody grabbed on in front of her.

"Maybe next time you won't blunder ahead like a blind mule." Annie said as Melody dug her heels into the snow and they pulled with all their might. They fell backward in the snow and kept pulling, but Brandon barely moved.

"Aw! My feet are going numb. I feel like an icicle. Pull harder!"

Annie heard movement in the snow behind her while she pulled. Two boots dug in on each side of her.

"Pull!" Garret's voice said from behind her.

Annie's heart suddenly felt like a lump in her throat. Despite her surprise, she dug in even harder and they all pulled together. Brandon moved! Annie was both relieved and strangely nervous with the prince sitting so close. She heard another person dig in behind Garret.

"Pull!" Garret ordered.

This time there was a huge new force on the rope and Brandon popped halfway out of the slush. They kept pulling together on Garret's command and soon Brandon was pulled to safety and shivering at their feet.

Garret spoke into his headset, "Medic squad, code blue hypothermia – Get the shuttle over here fast."

The tall muscular guy had to be Rick. He had been the last person on the rope. Removing the rope, Rick tried to haul Brandon up to get him on his feet, but he collapsed back into the snow.

Curt arrived with a thermal heated blanket to put around him.

Brandon was pale and shaking. "Aw man! My legs won't move." Brandon spit snow out through his chattering teeth. Garret's friends pulled him back to his feet. He slumped in their arms with the color drained from his face.

Most of the unit was by then gathered and Master Jordan had set the shuttle down nearby.

"Rick," Garret ordered, "get Brandon to the shuttle—fast." Rick and Curt quickly got Brandon's arms over their shoulders and plowed their way through the snow, following a safe trail of footprints. Medics ran to the shuttle ahead of them.

It all happened so fast. Annie found herself standing quietly next to Garret while he talked to Master Jordan on his headset. After some discussion, it was decided that the rest of the landing party should complete the exercise before returning to the ship. Brandon's limp body was carried up the ramp and into the shuttle. Melody's worried eyes turned to Annie. Frozen tears were on her cheeks. *Brandon needs to learn that his over confidence and lack of concern for himself can put others at risk.*

Annie reassured her. "It'll be okay, Mel. They're

trained to handle this kind of thing."

Garret stood at the center of the landing party, coiling the rescue rope. "Brandon will be fine as soon as he warms up. Now that you've seen what can happen, I shouldn't have to remind any of you to work safely as a team. Master Jordan wants every squad to keep scanning the surface. We don't want to lose anyone else. I'll join squad five. The rest of you fan out around the hot spring and stay focused."

Annie caught the petulant frown sent from Celia. It was the same look she always had when someone got in her way.

Melody led the way and scanned the ground. Garret lagged behind as he talked on his headset.

"I'm getting a life reading again," Annie reported and pointed the way. "Due east along the shore." Her scanner was glowing with life readings and the water in that direction was glowing blue. When she and Melody arrived at the edge of the pool, they saw something moving beneath the clear water. Small neon blue creatures darted about the crusty white rocks. They looked like glowing little seahorses. While most floated calmly, some had turned pink and started to zip and scurry about in alarm. Afraid to say anything aloud, Annie and Melody shared a look of excitement about their discovery and slowly kneeled down in the snow. Soon all of the seahorses were floating calmly and glowing with soft blue light.

Garret's face appeared in the surface of the water.

"Find something?" he asked. Suddenly, the seahorses turned pink. Water swirled about and they all disappeared.

"Well, we *did* find something," Annie said over her shoulder.

"Oh, sorry!" Garret said and backed away.

Melody looked at Annie and shook her head. "Guys!" she said in exasperation. "I'm going to look farther down along the edge. Maybe they didn't go far. Get a picture if they come back. Brandon will want to see this."

Annie smiled. Melody was always thinking about Brandon. Too bad he couldn't see how stuck she was on him.

"Was it something I said?" Garret asked.

"Mel just has this guy problem." Annie felt suddenly awkward looking at Garret. She struggled to refocus and kneeled down by the pool. She moved her gloved hand gently along the surface of the water hoping the seahorses would be curious.

"What are you doing?" Garret asked.

Annie shrugged and spoke softly, "Sometimes curious animals are drawn to gentle movements and sounds. I'm not sure why." She began to hum a soft tune. When Garret didn't move she peeked up and saw his dubious look. "I suppose you don't think it will work," Annie guessed.

"I didn't say that." His soft voice matched hers. There seemed to be something else on his mind.

"Where did you learn that tune?"

"Oh! It was something my mother use to sing."

Garret nodded. "I didn't think anyone sang those old ballads anymore." His curious smile curled up in a grin. "Well, don't fall in. I don't want to have to jump in after you. I'll be back after I check in with the others." He glanced back after he walked off with a curious look upon his face. He climbed a small rise to survey the area and checked on the landing team's progress.

Annie reached out to the bright blue water and began to softly hum. Her eyes searched the depths of the spring. A curious seahorse swam out into the open. She stopped humming and it disappeared. *It must have been drawn by the music.* She dug out her podcom from her jacket. She flipped it open, tapped a few buttons, and soft music began to play. Hoping she had found the right bait, she gazed again into the water.

Moments later she saw a flicker and something blue wiggled up into view. A few more seahorses joined the first one and began to glow. Soon there were dozens of little seahorses glowing brightly in the water. The music played on and the blue aura of sparkling mist grew brighter above the pool. Annie heard Melody step quietly up behind her. She turned, but froze when she saw who it actually was.

Garret's jaw had dropped. He had lifted off his goggles and Annie could see the excitement in his dark brown eyes. He grinned in amazement but he didn't say a word and kneeled down quietly beside her.

Annie's breath caught in her chest and her heart raced out of control. She was struck by the perfect contours of his flawless face, while he gazed into the glowing water. She hoped he couldn't see her staring through her dark goggles. She fumbled about until she located her podcom. She raised it up and snapped a picture of the pool with a flash of scanner rays. The blue aura suddenly turned pink and the pink seahorses darting for cover under the crusty white ledges of rock.

"I've never seen anything like that before," Garret said, breaking the silence.

"Neither have I," Annie admitted, looking at Garret. "I uh, suppose Master Jordan knew they were here." Her words tumbled out awkwardly.

"I'm sure he did," Garret said before he stood. "I believe our mission has been accomplished." He held out his hand and helped Annie to her feet. It was a simple gesture, which seemed natural to Garret. It was *unnatural* for Annie. Uncle Jordan was the only one who ever treated her like a lady. She hoped he didn't notice the flush of embarrassment she felt rush to her head.

The punching of boots through the snow, that announced Melody's return, broke the silence. "No signs of glowing anything!" Her frustration was punctuated by the rubbing of her arms for warmth. "I don't suppose they came back here."

"They did," Annie said and raised her datacom in

triumph. "We got proof."

"They did!" Melody's gasped in excitement and quickly closed the space between them. "Thank goodness," she said with a shiver. "My toes are froze. Let's go so we can show Brandon what we found."

"How are you going to explore other planets if you can't stand the cold?" Garret asked.

"Hello! Ship assigned communications specialist here."

Garret laughed as he repositioned his goggles and followed Brandon's trail back to the shuttle. He spoke into his headset to the rest of the unit. "All squad units report to the shuttle. This mission is now complete—. And uh—please watch where you step."

Annie hid a smile when she looked behind at Melody.

Melody's curious look suggested she wondered what had gone on between her friend and the prince.

Aboard the shuttle on the return flight, Brandon and the crew all viewed the picture of the seahorses on the holo-screen.

"A number of you were fortunate to see the *Lostradonyan luminos dociles*," Master Jordan said. "Commonly called the armored seahorse, these ancient creatures were once thought to be extinct. Only recently were they rediscovered in the hot spring. I fear they will soon succumb to the icy temperatures that affect the heated pools. Since they do not provide us with a food source, rescue efforts are not a priority for this species. It will be remembered as the first species brought by the ancient Netheans to adapt and persevere in the hostile north. My hope is that this experience gave you a taste of what you may find on other planets in the future. We should all be saddened by the loss of such fragile and beautiful creatures. But, we should also be heartened by the courageous rescue of our friend, Brandon. The efficiency of his rescue under our royal prince's command is to be commended. Take heart in what you have accomplished today. The dangers and discoveries in your future will be far greater." Master Jordan sat down and the students were left to wonder what the future would bring.

The unit of trainees arrived at the Starseeker station and departed from the launch bay. Survival training units from other shuttles passed them by. Most wore their Arctic survival gear but there was one sweaty unit in desert gear, with tanned and sun burnt faces. *Where on Treya could they have been?* Annie wondered. Brandon was still wrapped in a blanket when he walked to the launch bay repair shop.

"What a day!" Melody said, after she caught up with Annie. "Brandon seems fine now. He went to tell his dad his version of what happened before he hears it from someone else."

Annie laughed. "I'm sure he's feeling pretty dumb and hoping he didn't blow his chance for a mission assignment."

"Yep, you know him pretty well." Melody gave her a sidelong glance. "Are you sure there's nothing going on between you two?"

"I am positive." Annie found her friend's playful question amusing. "I'm afraid that floppy haired genius is all yours."

When they finally entered their squad bay, Melody heaved her bag of gear on the table and selected something from the food dispenser. "I can't wait to climb into my nice warm bed."

Annie yawned. "I feel like I could sleep for a week." She opened the door to her room and froze. Her clothes, sheets and pillows had been tossed about. Someone had ransacked her room.

11

ROYAL STABLES
DAY 7

SHUTTLES FLEW OVER THE CALDARIN MOUNTAINS following curved *vectronic* paths into their secluded green valley. Garret stood at the large tinted window watching the shuttles come and go. He was just one of many nobles looking for solitude at the King's Lodge. The top floor with glass walls belonged to the king of Gosar.

Prince Garret's thoughts strayed while his gaze fell into the rolling meadows of grazing horses. Tomorrow he would be crowned the heir of the most powerful kingdom on Treya. He feared his inherited duty and his father had sent him to the lodge to calm his nerves, yet there the king sat on his virtual throne for a visit. The holovision of King Fynlon Olsgood flickered.

"Lieutenant Curt," King Olsgood asked. "Have you completed your research of the royal family tree?"

"Yes Your Majesty," Curt reported.

Fynlon announced, "The time has come for my son to choose a wife. Have you also completed the list of noble born maidens?"

Prince Garret's attention snapped back to his father. "You're kidding, aren't you?"

To answer him, the king simply stated, "The heir to the Gosar kingdom has traditionally taken a queen by the age of 21."

Garret's amusement vanished. "You're not kidding, are you?"

"Curt," the King continued. "I chose you to find a suitable princess. I trust your skills will lead Garret to the perfect queen."

"Curt is going to pick my wife?"

"The woman must be of a suitable age from the ancient royal line of Nethas."

"It's just a tradition," Garret protested. "I thought if I fell in love I could chose who I wanted."

King Olsgood thumped his fist on the arm of his chair. "Choosing a queen must be approached with reason. It is expected by the people for you to marry a woman of royal birth. Your authority would be suspect if you don't. Tradition is what binds the authority of a kingdom. It isn't like there are only homely old spinsters to choose from. I insist that the woman must also prove herself to be kind and generous. But I fear this will exclude many of the young women I have seen at court."

Garret had sunk into a sulking mood. He knew he wouldn't win this argument. "If we're making a shopping list, it wouldn't hurt if she was pretty." He again turned away to look out the window.

Curt bowed to the king. "If I may ask, Your Highness, Why me? I'm sure there are many who serve you who would make a better matchmaker than I would."

"It must be you because it is you he trusts, and who he will listen to. I trust you have searched the family line and found all the female descendants close to his age. You will have Garret review it completely before the night of his crowning."

The king turned to Garret. "My little prince has grown into a fine young man. I do this only to help you. You know your mother and I only wish the very best for you."

Garret did not respond and continued to stare out the window.

"Very well," the king said as if all were now in order. "I leave you to your solitude until tomorrow," The king said and his image quickly faded away.

Curt ventured to ask, "Would you like to look at the list now or later. Some of them really aren't bad."

"Later!" Garret's jaw was set in defiance. "Let's ride first."

Rick who had been sitting relaxed in the corner jumped up ready to ride. Garret's two older guards rolled their eyes they knew the ride wouldn't be slow.

"Very well Your Highness," Curt said with a bow. "We'll reserve the evening for study."

Annie jumped from rock to rock beside a stream rushing down the mountain. Nearing the foot of a crashing waterfall, she found a path of boulders across the stream. Leaping water sprayed up all around her while plummeting water bounded over the stones. She paused to close her eyes and spread her arms in a spot of sparkling light. A tingling, cool spray showered over her arms and face. Contentment filled her as she listened to the tumbling water.

She climbed about wrapped in the mist and sound of rushing water. The rest of the world seemed no longer to exist. A bird chirped on a branch of flowers that hung over the bank. When she drew near, the bird fluttered up in a shaft of light and she was caught in a shower of petals. Annie picked up one of the delicate flowers. It smelled sweet and she placed it behind her ear.

In a few days her training would end. Missions to explore other planets could last for years or a lifetime. *Will I ever return here?* She wondered.

The warm rays of morning light had driven away the nervous confusion of her miserable night. Several other rooms had also been ransacked and security had been posted. Nothing of value was taken but in the disarray, her hairbrush and a few minor things were missing. *I can't believe someone was touching and tossing my things around?* To imagine it made her skin crawl.

The prying intruder reminded her of the odd questions from the man in black. There was no reason to believe she was in danger, but Uncle Jordan seemed on edge when he said not to worry and his creased brow told her he was keeping something from her. She suspected this trip to a secure place was his way of keeping her safe.

The whinny of a horse brought her back from her thoughts. She decided to rejoin her uncle downstream. She hopped along the rocks beside the water that tumbled down into a pool below.

Uncle Jordan sat on a mossy ledge by the clear pool, shaded by palms and ferns. He was reading an old book covered in leather while he ate meal cakes made from *stram.* Two horses on a tether grazed in nearby trees on the lush green forest undergrowth.

"Have something to eat before we ride back," Uncle Jordan said when Annie approached.

"What fascinating tale from the ancient realm are you reading now?"

Her uncle grunted with amusement. "How did you know?"

Annie grinned. "There is nothing else you enjoy doing more." She pulled on her loose, tawny riding pants up and over her shorts. She rolled up the sleeves of her loose white shirt that billowed above the wide waistband. Uncle Jordan wore the same white shirt and dark blue pants he always wore.

She nibbled a stram cake and ate some dried fruit. "My favorite story is the one about the huntsman and the spear maiden. My father use to read it when I was small." She pulled on her tall riding boots. "When they died their spirits were sent to the heavens to form constellations of stars. Legend claims the two constellations point to the shores of Kasaldune."

Uncle Jordan put on the jacket he left hanging up on a tree. "Kasaldune in ancient Calderian refers to a land of peace. A place that all people dream of."

Annie collected the food that remained and returned it to the saddle bags.

Uncle Jordan handed Annie the worn leather book. "A gift of stories from long ago."

"But they're your favorite," she objected.

"And I know them all by heart," he said before he kissed her forehead.

"Thank you, Uncle Jordan." She carefully put the book in her saddle bag. "I'll treasure it always." They both mounted their horses to return to the lodge.

Thundering hooves drummed the narrow path below as the mane of the white horse whipped at her face. Massive bones and muscle moved rhythmically to carry her in flying strides. Tall stalks of stram beside the path danced in rustling waves when the large horse split the wind. Annie turned in the saddle and saw that her uncle's small mare had fallen far behind. She reined in the gait of her mount and fought the stallion for his head.

When Uncle Jordan drew near he smiled. "Your skills at a cantor have greatly improved. Not long ago I was the one waiting for you, hoping you wouldn't fly out of your saddle."

The small mare fell into a brisk walk beside the stallion as the trail widened near the stables.

"I wasn't that bad." Annie hesitated. "Well, I don't cling on with my eyes shut anymore." She laughed with the memory of her first attempts at a cantor.

Riding a horse was part of a well-rounded education, according to her Uncle Jordan. The stables of Caldera housed most of the prized mounts from the frozen kingdoms of the north and south. Not all of the kingdoms could afford Nethian environment shields. Since there was no longer a place for horses in the icy regions, Caldera became a haven for valued breeds. Most royals were unable to travel on a regular basis to Caldera. They entrusted Master Jordan and a select few to exercise their prized possessions, in their absence.

"Maybe I'm ready to ski the giant downhill in Sakworth – with my eyes open this time."

"Maybe," Uncle Jordan said. His reserved laugh was skeptical.

They trotted through a grove of trees along the side of a meadow. Poles emitting beams of blue light guarded the edge of the field. Most animals knew to avoid the buzz fence. They slowed to a walk when the road turned to stone. Large green barns loomed up ahead. The sun glinted off the large barn that formed a "U" around a paddock.

The squeal of a horse suddenly rang out. Worry furrowed Uncle Jordan's brow. Annie's equally worried look sent them both in a gallop to the stable.

Jordan scanned his hand at a post outside the doors.

"Welcome, Master Jordan" an annoying robotic voice said through a speaker.

When the large doors slid open their horses leaped forward. The clatter of hooves over stone resounded high overhead. They slowed their pace when they merged with a crowd. Visitors and stable hands flowed through doors to the central paddock.

Over the circle of heads in a cloud of dust was a rearing black mass of muscle. It snorted and clawed at the air.

Annie removed her solar-shades and looked anxiously at Uncle Jordan.

Her uncle nodded his assent and took the reins of her horse.

She took a rope from the saddle and quickly dismounted. Calmly she walked through the crowd, toward the skittish horse in the center. She slowly climbed into the paddock and raised her open hands, still covered with riding gloves. A large angry stable hand fought for control at the end of a rope.

"Down, you cursed beast, or I'll whip your hide," he growled.

Annie looked steadily into the eyes of the horse as she walked. She could see the horse's fear in his flaring nostrils and in the white rings around his wide eyes. She began to quietly hum an ancient tune. It was not loud enough to be heard over the noise, but the angry horse twitched his ears towards her. She walked slowly up behind the stable hand, drawing the horse's gaze.

"Easy boy," she said softly. "No one wants to hurt you." *No one wanted to hurt him except maybe the man at the end of the rope,* she thought. The frightened horse wasn't ready to trust anyone. She took a firm grasp on the lead rope and leveled a commanding gaze at the man. "Drop it," she commanded.

For a moment he was caught in her fierce gaze. The rope gave a jerk and the man looked away. The man sneered with a laugh and said, "Fine – but the blame isn't mine when he kills you." He grinned with amused contempt and he released the rope.

The horse reared high up over her when he felt the anchor was gone. Annie lightly stepped away and let the rope slip free enough to let the horse have his own head. Quickly she clipped her rope to the end of the lead and started walking to the center of the ring. "Get him out of here," she ordered calmly. Some men stepped forward who looked happy to comply and escorted the angry stableman away.

"Easy boy, the bad man will be gone soon." She spoke quietly as if to calm a small child. He tried to bolt but the rope and fence forced him to circle. She spoke calmly and continued to hum. Pungent air wafted up from his sweaty hide when he bucked and shook his mane. His deep throated whinnies spoke of his rage and warned the onlookers to stay away. Gradually his speed and sudden changes in direction slowed. She took the rope in slowly and continued to gaze in his eyes. *I mean you no harm*, she thought while tilting her head from side to side. She did not wish to look threatening.

After a time, her humming became almost a whisper, while she walked calmly and held his gaze. She finally patted his neck gently and murmured reassuring praise. The crowd started to disperse. Annie slipped her sunglasses on and walked the stallion to a gate where another stableman took the lead.

"I'll take him for you, Miss. That was a brave thing you did. Old Clem sure got his – being showed up by a slip of a girl." He chuckled with pleasure and led the black stallion away.

Starseeker training in animal behavior can be useful, Annie thought and rejoined Uncle Jordan and the horses.

They left the paddock to water and brush down their mounts. A man tipped his hat and a woman bowed her head to Annie when she walked by. Annie's cheeks flushed with heat after she nodded in return and kept walking.

Where have I seen her before? Her face looked strangely familiar, Annie wondered. When they got to their stalls Uncle Jordan looked about and cautiously came to her side.

"You did a fine job calming the stallion." He then paused and his brows drew together. "I know you are in training to be a Starseeker officer, but you should be careful about assuming the authority to command others – though such a thing should not be surprising in a royal stable."

Annie nodded. Uncle Jordan always grew anxious when she drew attention to herself. She knew that both her aunt and he always tried to keep her out of public places. She didn't really know why. Uncle Jordan would only say that it was to protect her and that it was for her own good.

"Don't forget to check his hooves," he said before he returned to the next stall and began to brush down the mare.

The reminder about the hooves wasn't necessary. He had taught her how to care for horses many years ago. *I wish Uncle Jordan and Constance weren't always so protective*, she thought while she curried a few burrs from the tail of the tall stallion. Keeping her away from other people made her feel abnormal. The rare lavender colored flecks in her eyes made her avoid the gaze of others. It was no surprise that her aunt insisted she wear brown contacts or sunglasses.

She heard steps rustle through the sweet smelling straw. Knowing it was her uncle, she ignored his presence behind her.

Uncle Jordan then startled her when he looked over the high divider between the stalls. "I'm going to return my tack and speak with the head groomsman. I'll be back in a bit." He winked at someone behind her before he left.

Annie spun about and was startled to see Garret.

"I'm sorry," he said. "I didn't mean to startle you." He seemed uncertain about what to say. "I just wanted to thank you for calming my horse just now. It was certainly impressive how you—took control of the situation."

"You're welcome, Your Highness," Annie said with a nod over the back of her horse. "I was not aware it was your horse." Not knowing what to say to the prince of Gosar, she returned to brushing her own horse.

Garret appeared to relax when he leaned against the corner post of the stall. "I don't know why he bolted and threw me as soon as I sat in the saddle." He seemed to want a conversation, but didn't know where to begin.

Annie knew he expected some response. "No doubt there was a burr or something like it under the saddle pad." She frowned when she remembered the nasty little man. "Your groom didn't look like he knew or even cared about what he was doing. It doesn't look like you broke anything. You must bounce pretty well if your horse just threw you." She appraised his appearance and he really didn't look the worst for wear. He actually looked—well . . . . She couldn't finish her thought. She lowered her eyes to her work while warmth again rushed to her cheeks.

He must have sensed her discomfort because he also glanced down when half a grin crossed his face. "Yes, well—I was fortunate that my good friend Rick was nearby and practically caught me before I could hit anything—He has very quick reflexes."

Annie couldn't help but smile at the reserved charm he had used to deliver his amusing explanation.

After having to describe how his mount had unhorsed him, he shrugged nervously and shifted about. "We have never formally met. My name is Garret," he said and pressed his lips into a grin. "I'm sorry, I recall you from the Space Station, but I don't remember your name."

Annie smiled shyly. Because of his training in royal protocol to remember titles and names she suspected his forgetfulness was a ploy. He was obviously trying to be friendly. "My name is Annie." Some of the tension seemed to fall away while they looked at each other. She continued to go through the motions of her work but had no idea what to say. She had very little practice speaking to boys, and Brandon didn't really count.

"Do you ride here often with Master Jordan?"

Garret asked. He had slid quickly out of his ridged formality into a comfortable friendly manner.

"Yes," Annie said, thankful that he had spoken first. "Every seventh day we ride here, unless he finds another event to challenge me with." She grinned just thinking of Uncle Jordan's many unexpected trips.

"Interesting – and what other events has he taken you too?" Garret's face showed nothing but sincere interest.

"Well – ski jumping for one, and there's mountain climbing, and diving along coral reefs.

"I see," Garret responded with an amazed appreciation. "How long have you known Master Jordan?"

"Practically my whole life – He's like an uncle. He was my father's best friend." She felt a sudden sadness at the thought of her missing father. Garret must have noticed her changing mood and slipped back to his guarded formality.

"Well, I will have to enquire about doing some of those events myself – since he is my tutor." The stiffness was back. "I hope I may see you here again sometime, Miss Annie." He began an awkward retreat to the entry of the stall. "Thank you ever so much again for your assistance earlier—Good day, and please extend my greetings also to Master Jordan, and tell him I look forward to seeing him soon."

Annie was not sure how to respond to his formal request. "Sure," she said. "I'll let him know." She then added, "It was nice to meet you." The warm smile that broke over his face reminded her of just how handsome he was. She raised a hand in farewell and turned away before the warmth once again filled the skin of her cheeks. *Why did he come to talk to me?* She thought. *And why would I make him so nervous? Maybe he thinks I'm the daughter of a noble. I am in the stables of the king's horses—and his tutor had been with me—*. A sudden idea made her jaw drop. *The snob! He probably wouldn't even look at me if he knew who I really am.* She threw the grooming brush into a bucket.

Annie then overheard someone talking— "Well now that I know your type, it should be easy to pick a princess."

"Shhh! Not so loud you Oaf, it's not funny." The last voice sounded like Garret's.

Annie heard a shuffle of footsteps moving away. She looked out of the stall door and saw Garret returning to the other end of the stables with a group of men.

Picking a princess—know his type? What was that all about? Annie wondered. She quickly returned the brushes to the tack room at the end of the stables and was ready to go. She sat on a bale twisting straw in her hands while she waited for Uncle Jordan to return. *How many princesses were on his type list?* She searched the faces of those working in the barn. A young man with square shoulders not much older than her caught her eye. It was Garret, with his jacket removed and

133

brushing the back of his mount. He re-saddled his horse and adjusted the bridle. It was obvious he knew what he was doing when he checked one of the hooves. Garret looked up and saw her. She glanced away, embarrassed.

"Are you ready to go?" Uncle Jordan asked.

"Uh, yeah sure," she stammered. Garret was walking his horse their way, with four other riders behind him. It was no surprise when Uncle Jordan waved and walked over to greet Garret. Annie shyly followed at a distance.

"Good day to you, Garret. Are you all going out for a ride?"

"Yes." Garret said after he rolled his eyes towards the group that followed. "But don't worry. I'll be alone by the time I get back."

Master Jordan frowned and said, "You really shouldn't try to lose your friends."

"I know – but these old guys really aren't much fun to be around," he complained. Garret's attention turned to Annie, who was now standing behind her uncle. "Thanks again for calming my horse."

Master Jordan raised his brow. "It appears you two have gotten to know each other."

One side of Annie's mouth curled up before she addressed Garret. "You seem to know your way around horses."

"I've had an excellent teacher." He smiled at Master Jordan. His wristband then beeped. "I'm afraid

I need to get going. I got a late start. It was nice to have met you Annie. I promise I'll remember your name next time." He slyly nodded and urged his mount to move on.

"Remember your name?" Uncle Jordan asked.

"He didn't remember my name from the Starseeker Station."

Uncle Jordan frowned. "And I thought he was an intelligent boy."

12

HIDDEN PAST

THE STARSEEKER STATION was quiet when Annie returned that night. The lights were dim to begin the night rotation. She was tired, and planned to read from the book of legends her uncle had given her before the lights went off for the night. She was glad Celia and Tris were at home on Treya tonight. They wouldn't be back until after the crowning tomorrow. Turning down her corridor she found a tall man in uniform outside her quarters. *Who is it?* The violation of her room last night put her on edge. She summoned the same commanding tone she had used in the stables earlier and called out, "Who goes there?"

"Security Miss," the tall guard said. "We've been assigned to watch the cadet squad bays. No cause to worry, nothing's been going on here," he grinned.

His odd grin did not help take the edge off Annie's fear. *Should I trust him?* she wondered. Her heart quickened its pace. She reached out to scan her hand. The door whisked open and a shout rang out when a man's face appeared in the door.

"SURPRISE!" he said.

Annie felt like her heart jumped into her throat. She defensively raised her arms.

The floppy haired head, and big toothed grin of Brandon, had appeared in the door.

"Did I scare you?" he hopefully asked.

Annie slapped him in the shoulder. "I nearly jumped out of my skin. What are you doing here?"

The guard stifled a laugh.

"With a friend like you, who needs enemies?" Pushing past him, she saw his parents, Tad and Mirra Granger with Melody, and Uncle Jordan. *How did he get here so fast?*

"Happy Birthday!" they all shouted after she walked in the room. E-Chip whistled and played a birthday tune.

Mirra presented her with a extraordinary cake she had made. It was beautiful enough for a queen. Annie marveled at the intricate lace woven with strands of icing and the surface sparkled like fresh fallen snow. *What wonderful friends she had.* Tears rolled down Annie's cheeks.

"We couldn't let your sixteenth go by without wishing you well," Mirra said when she began to serve them cake. She could always depend on Mirra to show up for special occasions. Everyone groaned with delight over the delicious cake. Even the guard had been served a piece. The plates were whisked away by the recycle vacuum in the center of the table and were followed by the cups for punch.

"Thank you all for doing this." Annie beamed with a glowing smile. "But, aren't you a bit late?" Everyone became silent. Annie looked around. Something was up. "I mean—my birthday was several days ago."

"Yes," Uncle Jordan said. He sat down across the table from her. "There is something I've wanted to tell you for a very long time."

Brandon and Melody looked clueless at each other.

Uncle Jordan continued, "Today is your real birthday."

Annie's brow furrowed. *Real birthday? What is he trying to say? Why would my real birth date be different—or a secret?*

He pulled out a wrapped object and set it before her. "This will tell you everything you need to know."

Mirra explained, "Your mother told me to give you this on your eighteenth birthday. But, we decided it was time that you knew a few things." Mirra sat down beside her with a reassuring smile.

"This is from *Mom*?" Annie was stunned. E-Chip's visual sensors rose up on a post and zoomed in for a better view.

"Open it already!" Brandon said impatiently. She

carefully untied the ribbon and unfolded the paper to reveal a plain, slightly outdated comcord.

Tad stood up to stretch and yawn. "Well, we hate to eat and run but it really is late." His tired act was totally unconvincing.

"Yeah, I'm bushed!" Brandon's quick agreement was even *more* unconvincing. "It's been a long day."

Mirra sighed and shook her head. "I guess I need to go roll these two into bed," she chuckled. "Don't you stay up reading after lights-out."

"I'll be good, Mirra." Annie stood and gave her a hug. "Thanks for everything. I love you all." They said their good-byes and the door quietly slid closed behind them.

"What is this all about?" Annie asked her uncle.

Uncle Jordan pulled her to her feet and gave her a hug. "You're the closest thing I have to a daughter, Annie. There are some important things you need to know about yourself. But, it is better that you hear it from your mother. We'll talk tomorrow about what she has to say. Just remember you're safe. There are guards outside." He kissed her forehead and he too went out the door.

Melody looked at Annie with stunned curiosity. "Wow! I wonder what that was all about? *"Don't worry you're safe*, but from what? You better give me the scoop tomorrow—I want details." They hugged and she went off to bed.

Annie picked up her mother's comcord journal

from the table and headed for her sleep bay.

She showered off quickly and slipped into a night shirt. Sitting propped up in her bed, she raked her fingers through her wet hair and turned the journal on. The journal screen opened to a security wall.

That's unusual! Annie pressed her hand on the screen. The Nethas crest of two seahorses appeared on the screen. She clicked past it and was excited to see a holoscreen option. She tapped it and light projected outward when she laid the journal down on her lap. A fuzzy image flickered and resolved into the figure of her mother. Annie shivered when a tingle ran up her back.

The soft voice of her mother then spoke. "Hello, Annie! If you are listening to this it is either your sixteenth birthday – so happy birthday – or it was decided that it's time for you to know a few things. I'm sorry I'm not there to tell you what you need to know, myself."

Annie reached out as if to touch her mother's face. It had been so long since she had seen her mom. Her eyes welled with tears.

"Much happened before you were born that you should know," her mother began. "So you may understand, I will start at the beginning." Annie strained forward as adrenaline pumped into her veins.

"Nethas was the first and only kingdom of Treya for thousands of years. But the kingdom grew chaotic and battles were fought during a time when most of our technology was lost. Sons of the royal family departed and established new kingdoms around the world. The Nethian rulers were peaceful and wise. But some have strayed from the ancient ways.

The kingdom of Gosar grew in trade and rediscovered some technology. Over the centuries, its power to sway decisions surpassed Nethas. There was no war, it was simply time that shifted the power of world leadership to Gosar.

King Kretus of Omara rules a neighboring kingdom to Nethas. He believes the rule of Treya rightfully belongs to Nethas. Radicals that support him have grown in number. They no longer want to bow to the Gosar King and the Council of Kings who direct the battle against the ice age. King Olsgood of Gosar is a kind and wise ruler.

My father believes it is the duty of Nethas, as a leading kingdom, to inspire world unity. Division in crisis only brings destruction." The image of her mother smiled, "Dad always did play the heavy. If you ever get to know him, you'll find he's really an old softy underneath." She paused. Her smile left and she became serious.

"I am the daughter of Gythos and Inowa Franchini, the King and Queen of Nethas. That makes you a princess to the throne of Nethas . . . ." Annie stopped the recording and replayed the last line. A tingling sensation washed through her, and her jaw dropped in bewildered confusion.

"I know this will come as a surprise," her mother's holovision went on to say. "But, you must know it was imperative to keep your identity hidden.

I had two brothers who died. Some suspect they did not die by accident. I am my father's only heir to the throne. If something happens to me and my children, the rule of Nethas passes to Kretus. His family is our closest link on the royal family tree.

Special Guardians were assigned to me. One of them was your father, Bryan. The Guardians stopped several attempts on my life before they changed my identity." Her mother's face grew sad. "I miss being able to see or talk to my parents, but I know we are safer in hiding until the radicals are suppressed.

Ellen Pierson is my cover name. My real name is Dania Elaina Franchini and your real name is Angelina Franchini Roeshell. I changed my name when I secretly married and went into hiding on the Starseeker Station with your father. An accident was staged to make it look like we were dead. You would think that we gave them what they wanted, but in reality we have protected the future heir of Nethas, and that is you."

Staged death? Annie took a deep breath as she tried to take it all in. *The history of royalty was familiar except all the Franchini heirs are thought to be dead. It's so unreal. How can I possibly be involved in royalty and heirs to a throne?*

The recording continued, "Hand scans on the

Starseeker station don't register on Treya's data stream because of security. Changing my scan identification from royalty to a Starseeker crew member was a simple matter. When you were born, you were not identified as a princess of Nethas. No one knows you exist, but you must not draw attention. There was a rumor for a time that I was alive and had a child.

Though our false identities are secure on the Starseeker station you were given a different birth date for the records. We believe the enemy of Nethas still searches for the rumored child, so you must never let your hand be scanned on the planet's surface. An undocumented citizen of your age would draw attention. An eye scan will reveal that you are the offspring of royalty and will give you admittance anywhere without identifying you, but it can still be dangerous."

That's why Uncle Jordan always steered my hand clear of scanners. He and who else knows? My overprotective Aunt Constance—my father's sister? She must know.

"First," her mother continued, "you may have noticed that no one else has the same colored eyes as you do. Lavender-blue eyes are a mark of royal heredity, but that is not commonly known. Second, never let anyone take samples of your blood or hair. These can identify your genetic heritage."

"It's all too much!" Leaving the journal playing on her bed Annie got up and started pacing about her small quarters. *Maybe that's why I couldn't find my hairbrush after the break in. I'll have to tell Uncle Jordan.*

"I don't know if King Kretus himself wants us dead, but Omara fanatics would kill or try to get rid of us to gain the Kingdom of Nethas."

Kill us! Kill me? Annie leaned into the wall opposite her bed and melted down to the floor.

"We've taken precautions against possible sabotage of our mission. It is highly unlikely, but recent events suggest that someone may suspect who I am. Jordan, Constance, Mirra and Tad all know what I've told you and are sworn to secrecy and your protection."

Mirra and Tad too. Is there anyone else hiding me?

"Your father and I love you very much. I know you'll be safer with Jordan and Constance than with us for now. My hope is that I will see you very soon. If we are unable to return, there should be enough information with Starseeker Command for a rescue mission, but if you're listening to this that didn't happen. Remember, you can always trust Jordan in all things and keep E-Chip safe." The recording broke off and fuzzed out—but the image reformed and her mother reappeared in a soft tan flight suit.

A message followed that was garbled. "One last thing—th$_{er}$$^{e's}$ $_a$ ... $^{\#}/\sim//\#$ ... $_{om}$ E-Chip stored in th ... $^{\#}/*^{/}/\#$ ... $_{or}$ constructing star charts $^{th}_{at}$ will lo^{-o}cate Tamaroon. Only you can access this recording and I can't think of a safer place to leave it."

Star charts? Where?

A soft warning tone sounded in Annie's cabin and the lights went out. The holovision glowed even brighter in the dark.

"E-Chip holds the key to find the star-trail to Tamaroon. So keep him safe in case something should happen."

A little girl ran into the picture and jumped at her mother's feet.

"Mommy, Mommy," a younger Annie said, and grabbed her mother's legs when something growled.

Her father entered the image. "I'm going to get you," he said playfully before he scooped her up in his arms and tickled her. Turning to her mother he asked, "Are you done? We have to go."

"Yes, I'm done," she kissed her father on the cheek. "I'm just leaving a message for Annie to play later. You know just in case"

"Your mother is such a *worry wart*." Her father turned and waved at the camera. "Say good-bye to the camera Annie."

"Good-bye!" the little girl laughed.

The holo-image disappeared and she was alone in the dark. She sat frozen while the recognition of the event she just saw flashed in her mind. Her mother's warnings swirled about in her thoughts—*Sabotage? fanatics?* She knew now why Uncle Jordan said they would talk tomorrow. She crawled back into bed with the journal and replayed the vision of her mother and her warnings over and over. The aching hole in her chest had reopened and it was a long time before her eyelids grew heavy with sleep. She finally opened a niche with a pass code over her bed and put the comcord on top of the book of legends. She rolled over and closed her eyes against the tears. *I will find a way to Tamaroon.*

13

SECRET GUARD

THE STARSEEKER GUARD saluted when Commander Jordan passed and entered his office. It was earlier that same day before Jordan flew with Annie to the stables. "Secure door," he commanded. The ship responded and a second door dropped over the doorway. Tad, Mirra, Constance and several Starseeker officers were already seated behind his desk. "Thank you all for coming," he said and checked the time on his podcom. "The others should be here soon." Jordan sat behind his desk with his back to them.

A glowing light in the air before them, formed into a holographic royal guard. He bowed, examined the small room and floated off to one corner. He quietly reported that all was secure on his podcom. Other holographic figures arrived in a similar fashion. Their images blended together as they multiplied and moved to the edges of the small room. The gathering display of uniforms represented royal guards from the seven major kingdoms. The ancient Guardians, hidden in the royal guard, were highly trained agents bound to protect the royal kingdom. Last to arrive in the center of the room was King Fynlon Olsgood of Gosar, and King Gythos with Queen Inowa Franchini of Nethas. The queen's presence was a surprise and a quite stir of comments rose from the assembly.

Commander Jordan stood to bring order and address them. "Thank you all for coming." He bowed to king Olsgood, the commander of the secret Guardians, and the Nethian rulers. "Your Majesties."

"Yes, yes," King Olsgood said impatiently. "Get on with it. What is so important that you called a gathering of the Guardians?"

"It's Angelina, Sire." Jordan said with a bow of his head. "I fear she has been discovered by the Dark Knights." Inowa joined hands with Gythos in concern.

"What evidence do you have?" King Fynlon asked.

Commander Jordan outlined what the Guardians had discovered. "Six days ago, your son's body guards identified a black knight in the cadets defense training gym. Four days ago, Angelina was the last cadet to be questioned by a dark knight during the shuttle race investigation; and two days ago, five cadet rooms were searched but none more than Annie's. These incidents along with increased movement and communication among the Dark Knights, may indicate they are planning a show of force. Tomorrow, all the royal families of Treya will be gathered for the crowning of the heir to Gosar. A surprise attack at this event would be devastating."

"The crowning is always well protected by the Guardians," Inowa offered.

"Yes, and King Kretus and his Dark Knights know it," Gythos said. "They also know Angelina must claim her birthright to the public within thirty days of her sixteenth birthday, or our family line to the Nethas throne will legally come to and end. His deeply furrowed brow drew together.

"We will triple our forces!" Fynlon growled. "Falling into war would threaten our survival. If the rule of Nethas by the house of Franchini were to end, war would follow. There must be a strong defense to keep the rebels at bay tomorrow. Everything depends on us establishing a steady source of food and heated dwellings. There should be no question in their minds of the outcome if they were to attack." His passion to defend Treya held no love for the blindly selfish rampage of a barbarian.

Jordan added, "Since the Dark Knights have already made Angelina a target, we should reveal her to the people. They would think twice before executing a newly discovered heir to the throne of Nethas."

"Her assassination would bring war." There was dread in the face of Gythos and many others.

"Which is why a large show of force should be

clear," Fynlon agreed.

"I suggest that Angelina attend the royal ball as the Princess of Nethas," Jordan proposed.

"Wouldn't that expose her to danger?" Inowa said. Her hands clung tight to the arms of her throne.

"She is in worse danger if we do not," Gythos said. He placed a reassuring hand on hers.

"If she is not revealed, the Dark Knights could kill her without the people ever knowing she exists," said Fynlon.

"We will have the advantage with an increased force of the secret Guardians," Jordan said with confidence.

"As head of the ancient Guardians of the allied kingdoms, let it be so," Fynlon proclaimed.

"Very well, Sire," Jordan bowed. "I hereby alert all Guardian Forces to prepare for the ball, when Angelina Franchini Roeshell will be revealed as heir to the throne of Nethas. This meeting is adjourned."

King Olsgood and the multitude of holographic images quickly phased out. A face belonging to Curt, Garret's guard, disappeared with them.

Commander Jordan turned to the Starseeker officers present. "Instruct the Guardians in your command to detain anyone suspected of spying or working for the Dark Knights, dismissed!"

The officers quickly departed.

Jordan turned to Tad and Mirra and smiled. "We will meet tomorrow as planned."

They returned smiles of relief and excitement. "All will be ready," Mirra assured him. They also left Jordan's office.

Constance looked at Jordan with a tear in her eye and concern etched in her face. "She'll be all right, won't she?"

Jordan hugged her with much affection. "We have done all we can for her safety, my love. An alliance between Nethas and Gosar would be a great advantage to the allies. I am eager to see young Garret's face when he meets our Princess."

Garret was again feeling caged by his position as the future heir to a throne. He stood looking out the high window of his apartment. He longed to be free to roam the green pastures that spread below. The control others had on his life was so confining that they now threatened to determine when and whom he would marry.

Rick sat relaxed at his station scanning the security log. The review of princesses had not been going well and Curt had decided they all needed a break. When Curt returned to the room, he whispered quietly to Rick. Sitting up straight, Rick appeared to double his effort on his security sweep. Garret had remained brooding by the window.

"Are you ready to continue the review?" Curt asked cautiously.

Garret reluctantly turned from the window. He knew it was useless to argue with his father, the King. He returned to the viewing screen with Curt. Sitting with resignation, he leaned on the arm of his plush chair.

Curt was aware of his mood. "Perhaps this would be easier, Your Highness, if you were to realize there are people like Rick and I who can't date or marry because of our job."

Curt's comment got Garret's attention. He had never thought about their duty to him as a burden that kept them from a life of their own. "I'm sorry, I . . . ."

"No, Your Highness, I wasn't looking for pity. The reason I pointed this out is, if you could try to look at this as an opportunity, it wouldn't seem so hard."

Garret could see his loyal guard was trying to help him. "I'll try," he said with sincerity.

"I tried to find every unwed girl of royal birth close to your age. I'll continue to present them in no particular order, Your Highness. Who you eventually marry will be for you to decide. So, please stay open to the possibility they might be interesting. I'll continue to cross off those definitely not in the running." Curt sat in a chair by the Prince. "Screen on," Curt commanded. A holo-screen image of a royal born candidate appeared.

"Princess Certa Kandora of Sethaly," Curt read aloud.

"It says she's twenty-five," Garret responded. "You call a girl seven years older than I am, close in age. She's a no."

Princess Linna Procovich of Hincort," Curt read.

Garret's repulsion was obvious. "I've met her. She talked of nothing but the newest fashion and gossiped about everyone. She's a definite no."

Princess Corina Duchark of Caldera," Curt said.

"She's just a kid," Garret said in disbelief. "How did she make the list?"

"She's fourteen," Curt explained. "By the time you're twenty-one she'll be seventeen."

"Fine," Garret relented. "Leave her on the list."

"Princess Dania Franchini of Nethas," Curt read. An attractive young woman with long blonde hair appeared on the screen.

Garret paused while he looked at her picture. He read the information displayed beside it. "Why is she listed as missing?" He asked. "I thought all the Franchini heirs died."

Curt explained, "There is a rumor that she may still be alive . . . ."

"Wait a minute," Garret interrupted. "According to her date of birth she should be thirty-seven years old. Even if you could find her, she is old enough to be my mother. I think that qualifies her as a definite *no*."

"Sorry," Curt apologized. "Her most recent picture made her look young." Curt smiled and seemed to judge Garret's first impression as favorable towards a Franchini princess.

The review continued until only a small number of candidates remained on the list. None of them seemed to fit Garret's idea of a girl he wanted to live with—let alone marry. He slumped in his chair. *Tomorrow I'll meet them all as contenders trying to win me as a prize.* The image of a girl singing in the snow next to a misty pool lingered in his mind.

14

DARK KNIGHT

KING KRETUS SARVOK FUMED angrily in his nephew's face. "Four years, and you haven't learned where that cursed planet is," Gillo stood his ground, but cringed from the expected blow that never came. He didn't dare respond until Kretus had paced away to a safe distance. *Why did I cringe?* he thought. *My uncle has never hit me before.*

Kretus slumped heavily into a studded leather chair. He gulped down the dark ale in his mug and his smoldering gaze settled on the fireplace. Somber light from the flickering flames danced about in the dark chamber. The pointed ears of his two hounds relaxed in the silence, but their eyes remained alert while they cowered at his feet.

Gillo sat in a chair by the fire to watch the wavering flames. When his uncle's face had mellowed he spoke. "Such information is not easily found,

Uncle."

Dancing light from the fire reflected in the king's eyes as he seemed to consider his words.

"The Starseeker Station security has many layers and backup systems," Gillo explained in defense. "They are strongest around Master Jordan's office and sleep bay. The old fool has taken great care to hide anything of worth. My search there found nothing."

Gillo watched the king's brooding face simmer in the firelight. "Those miserable Guardians think they know what is best for our world." His deep voice rumbled like an angry bear. "They continue to hide truth from the people. I know that missing planet is a key to something bigger than others suspect, and they refuse to talk about it." Kretus slammed his fist into the arm of his chair. His eyes burned beneath the shadow of his brow. "I've been much too patient waiting for the old Nethians to pass on my birth right. The kingdom of Nethas belongs to me."

Gillo sipped from his own mug and cautiously avoided his uncle's eyes.

Kretus drank deeply and looked out the icy window at the snow-covered town below. "If my grandfather had not found those weather control center plans in our family archives, and experimented out of curiosity, it wouldn't be like this. In his hands it perfectly controlled the growing seasons. There were bumper crops of every kind for all the kingdoms. Money flowed like sweet honey through every hand.

Even the poorest farmer became wealthy. Confound my father and his brainless minions for corrupting its programming. He's the one who caused the thirty years of growing famine and death." Kretus tipped his mug only to find it empty. "Ajax, more ale, man. Don't you know when my mug is dry?"

"Pardon me Sire! I can be such a buffoon." Ajax stepped from the shadows with a decanter to fill the king's mug.

"You are no buffoon, Ajax. You are the only one I truly trust." Kretus continued to brood. "My father was like a god who could do no wrong when I was young. My brother was always his favorite. Did you know that, Gillo? Even after your father's shuttle crashed when you were a babe, my father didn't treat me like him."

Gillo's thumb ran over the scar down the side of his face from the crash. He had never known his parents. The cruel looking scar reminded him of their loss every time he looked in the mirror.

The sinister glower on Kretus' face melted into a wistful expression. "My sweet Elaine loved me though. How could she have left me when I offered her the world?" A sad expression drew together his ruffled brow. He sipped from his mug and stared at nothing.

Gillo had never heard him speak of his wife before. He was surprised by the depth of feeling etched in his uncle's face.

His uncle's tender memory was brief and his

mood suddenly soured. "Did you know the shift in the weather pattern is permanent?" He scowled at Gillo. "My engineers have found no way to end the cycle of snow and ice. Instead of inheriting power over world trade, my father has made me the master of destruction." Kretus sniffed at the loss of living his grandfather's dream.

"My father caused the people to cluster in the kingdom strongholds. But, it has made them become weak and compliant. If my father had known, he would have caused the weather shift much sooner." Kretus laughed at the thought. "We could have convinced our sleepy sheep of Omara by now, that Nethas should be joined with us."

Gillo obediently remained quiet while his uncle ranted on. Nothing ever good came from speaking without the King looking for your response. After years away from the castle, he could now see the sinister intent in his uncle's incautious desire for power. He understood now why his subjects feared him.

Gillo, my boy!" Kretus looked at him with narrowed eyes. "I'm going to trust you with a secret." He leaned forward although there was no need. "My advisor has discovered the weather station was originally designed and operated on another planet. Old legends say it died long ago and that it was called Tamaroon." Kretus smiled wide. "Can you believe that?"

Gillo couldn't imagine such a thing being true.

Ajax shifted uncomfortably in his corner.

"Ajax discovered that my grandfather somehow got the plans to control the weather from the ancient kings. He passed them on to my father, but my father's sudden death prevented him from telling me where he hid them." Kretus took a deep breath, "However, my security agents have learned that a rumored child of the commander who found Tamaroon may know where the missing star charts are."

Gillo was caught short. *Does he seriously plan to fly to some lost planet?*

"If you and I can find those star charts to this missing world and learn how to fix and control the blasted manipulation of the weather." He smiled with golden flames glinting in his eyes and in a deathly hush of silence he proclaimed, "We will have the wealth of Treya at our feet."

15

TRACK TUBE

DAY 8

ANNIE'S WRISTBAND BARKED, "Up, up, up! First rotation will soon begin! Dress right and look sharp. Visiting officers are on board . . . ."

Annie shot up from a dead sleep. Realizing she was safely sitting on her bed, she dragged her hand down over her face. She recalled the message from her mother which made her happy, sad, curious and afraid all at the same time. The turbulent storm of emotion raged in the pit of her stomach. Dazed with renewed grief she retrieved and replayed the end of her mother's journal several times. Her parents looked just as she remembered them. *I'm a princess of Nethas that no one knows about? Why did they not tell me? I need to talk to Uncle Jordan. There was a garbled message about star charts. It must lead to the charts I've been looking for.*

AMARIS, I must see Master Jordan as soon as

possible.

Master Jordan is currently occupied. You will be notified when he becomes available.

AMARIS continued, "Please report in ten tarpecs to track tube five on deck fourteen."

The familiar voice was agitating, yet strangely comforting. There was nothing she could do except follow her assigned duty. *Visiting officers?* she groaned, *it just means look busy all day.*

Annie stretched and rolled out of bed with the journal. Her dreams had been full of dark shadows chasing her through endless corridors.

"Where should I hide this?"

E-Chip beeped recognizing a question. He sent a message stream across her pod screen. "Hide it under your bed with Garret's picture."

When Annie read the text, she frowned with annoyance that E-Chip had seen her do that. "Like that would be secure." *After ten years I get a secret warning from my mother? I still can't wrap my head around the princess part.* She pressed several buttons and returned it to her wall locker. "I'll come up with a better place later." She switched out of her nightshirt into a streamlined suit with padded knee and elbow pads. Over that, she slipped on her flight jacket.

AMARIS sounded a final reminder. "Four tarpecs to track tube five."

"I'm on it!" Annie pulled her hair up in a clip, locked AMARIS on her wrist and jammed on her eyewear. "See you at study time E-Chip. Hold the fort while I'm gone."

E-Chip whistled and beeped as he moved into position by the door.

Annie arrived in plenty of time on deck fourteen. New security patrols were everywhere. She noticed two were stationed near the entry to the track. She tried to pretend it had nothing to do with her and her new found heritage. Anxious to leave her troubled thoughts behind, she scanned her hand by the door and escaped into the cool air of the warm-up chamber. The small rubber floored room had a bench on each side and at the far end was the clear wall of the track. While she stretched her legs, she heard a rapid thumping that grew louder and faster in the tube.

A gliding figure rumbled up over the breaking ridges in the tube floor. The door opened for Melody and she entered breathing hard on wobbly legs. She dragged her feet like heavy weights to the bench where she collapsed. Her skin glistened with sweat.

"You know you shouldn't sit down right away," Annie remarked, while she strapped on roller-bar boots.

Melody responded with a sidelong glance. She then hung her head between her knees. "I am sooo ready for a shower," she moaned.

"I thought I had an early track time," Annie said when she stood. "I'll talk to you later Mel."

"Hey wait up!" Melody called, "You haven't told

me about your mom's journal yet. Have you read it?"

Annie shrugged. "You know I tell you everything. I'll see you at lunch. But just keep this between us." She paused and added, "And of course Brandon."

Melody blushed.

Annie stepped onto the track as her friend sank back in disappointment. She closed the tube hatch, which fit perfectly into the streamline wall. Her gliding steps inside the tube soon stretch out into long thrusting strides. Annie gathered speed as she circled the hollow interior of the Starseeker station.

There were ten track tubes in all that followed the walkways on open levels of the station. Other track runners were also beginning their workouts.

As her speed picked up, the gravitational force carried her up the outer wall of the tube. She rested one arm behind her back while she swung the other arm in time with her stride. It wasn't long before the quarter lap sounded and Annie slid her feet sideways into the rising break ridges. She slowed quickly to a stop with one hand dragging. Using the traction on her toes she pushed off in the opposite direction. She and the others would repeat the turn twice before they could glide in to a halt.

The steady rhythm of Annie's stride, allowed her mind to wander. The news of her unknown heritage had her rattled. *Why didn't Uncle Jordan ever tell me?* The lost trust in the person she admired most now squeezed and wrenched at her heart. *He lied to me!* It was a lie by omission but it still stung like nothing she had ever known.

Her deep breathing made her aware of her growing emotion. The old bottled up hurt and anger of being left alone by her parents fed heat to the growing flames of rage.

Angry strides propelled her faster around the track. The turmoil of being angry at those she loved most made her anguished strides intense.

Annie barreled into the breaking ridges that rose in the track and skidded into a reverse turn. The heat of betrayal drove her toes into a rapid-fire take off that sent her flying back the way she had come. The protective wall built to hide feelings of being left alone, melted in a flood of hot tears. They streamed back along her face as she rushed head long through the curving tube.

Her parent's last parting, replayed in her mind for the billionth time. Her breath came hard and fast until she recalled the tears in her parents' eyes when they left. A sudden sadness washed through her and squelched the flames of anger.

"They didn't leave me on purpose," Annie heard herself say.

Her mother's holographic face flashed in her mind. The rhythm of Annie's stride slowed. She could hear the echo of her mother's warning. *"There are dangerous fanatics who would kill us—Someone may suspect who I am—and sabotage—our mission."* Her mother's words struck home. They had suspected all those years ago that they were in danger. That's why they told Uncle Jordan to keep her safe—with a secret identity. *Mom's the one who warned me not to scan my hand off the space station. That's why Uncle Jordan always took my hand and scanned his own—like that first time at Gosar palace.*

A Princess? Royalty? The idea of herself being a part of that world had always been beyond her. The only royalty she knew was Garret. Her stride slowed to an easy glide. *Do I really belong to his world now?* Her mother's words from the journal echoed in her mind. *"Your real name is Angelina Franchini Roeshell—You are the heir to the throne of Nethas—no one knows you exist."* Everything she had known and believed about herself seemed to turn upside-down. She was not just an orphaned nobody anymore, but instead the only heir to a throne, hidden from a danger she did not understand. *Why didn't Uncle Jordan ever tell me? I need to talk to him.*

Annie's feet rumbled over the breaking ridges. She dragged one foot for traction and glided to a stop.

The dark figure of a man stood watching by the door.

Fear caught in Annie's throat. It was the only way out. The door slid open and revealed two more men behind him.

"Am I really that scary?" Annie heard someone say. She looked up to find Garret's smiling face. "You look like you just saw a ghost."

A tingle of immense relief shuddered up Annie's spine as her dark thoughts were pushed back and contained. She wiped the tears from her face and took Garret's hand without thinking. For a moment in the warm-up chamber, her eyes held his. She then realized she was holding the prince's hand in front of Curt and Rick. Warmth flushed her cheeks. She timidly let go of his hand and stepped back.

Garret grinned. "I didn't know that was you in there. You built up a lot of speed. Was a Swordtooth Zorker chasing you?" he asked, before his hands pounced through the air. The prince and his friends seemed to be quite amused.

Annie's face scrunched up while she considered. "Hmm! Something like that." Fear of being hunted had not left and her serious response killed their fun.

"Well," Garret said. "I guess it's my turn to try this thing out."

Annie opened her mouth in surprise. "You've never tubed before? Didn't Master Jordan send you with an instructor?"

"Nah," Garret scoffed. "It doesn't look that hard."

What could Uncle Jordan have been thinking? she thought.

Garret's sure and steady feet clomped onto the track. He smiled and proclaimed. "My superior physical training as the Prince of Gooosar—Oooaf!" Garret's feet had flown out from under him and he landed with a forceful thump.

The look of surprise on his faced brought a titter of amusement from his friends.

Determination spread across Garret's face. "You know that I am not the moron I appear to be."

The amusement on the faces of Curt and Rick respectfully drained.

Annie was annoyed that the prince of Gosar sat clueless in an unfamiliar device without support or advice. "Use the edges of the boots for traction. Stand up on the toes and use them to start running to launch into rolling strides."

The encouragement in her words softened his defeated brow. "I know," he said with a wiry grin. "I did read the manual." He took a deep breath and with confident steps he rose.

The clear door closed and he took off in strong deliberate strides. Annie sat down and changed her boots.

Rick and Curt burst out laughing while they watched Garret's progress.

"It serves him right," Curt said. "He's always jumping into things, acting like he already knows everything."

Rick agreed. "He really is cocky! He thinks he can do everything himself, and he was always escaping from those old guards."

Annie felt like she just got a glimpse of what Garret's life was like. She stood and watched Garret's movement become more fluid. She spoke her thoughts half to herself, "I suppose a prince would be raised to be independent and think for himself." She then realized Curt and Rick were both looking at her. She hesitated, "I should be—on habitat duty. I guess I'll see you—around." She uncomfortably backed her way to the outer door and made her escape.

16

TAMAROON DOME

"WHY DID YOU NEVER TELL ME?" Annie asked. She fought the bitterness that caught in her throat. Uncle Jordan surely had some logical explanation. She had come to his office after her morning exercise, and told him what she learned from her mother's journal.

"It was for your own safety," Jordan explained. "You were never told because if you were questioned, you could truthfully deny everything."

"Does Aunt Constance know?"

"Yes!"

"How long has she known?"

"We have both known since the day you were born."

"Well, that explains a few things." Annie slumped in her chair. "She was always such an overprotective mother hen—and us living so isolated and alone." She grew intent and leaned forward. "How much danger am I in?"

"No one can truly say how much." Uncle Jordan sighed. "There are guards to protect you. If I thought you were in danger I would be at your door or by your side at all times. Try not to worry. I'll make sure you are safe."

Annie stood and began to pace about uneasily.

"How long am I to be hidden?"

"That too is unclear."

"Am I actually expected to rule Nethas some day?"

"Yes Angelina, you are the heir to the throne, and will one day rule Nethas."

"But I don't know anything about ruling a country."

"Ah, but you do! The only thing you haven't learned is how to issue orders to a domestic staff and make royal decrees."

"I don't believe you."

"You know how the world economy works. You know the history of all the major kingdoms. You have a solid foundation in law, morality, and what people need to prosper. Knowledge is the sound foundation on which any good decision is made. "

"But—!" Annie was at a loss for words.

"But what, your highness?"

"Don't call me that."

"It is your birthright. But as you wish, I will not use your title until you are ready."

The pent up steam in Annie seemed to dissipate when her pacing slowed and became less agitated.

"I don't feel much like a princess. Are you sure there's no mistake?"

"There's no mistake. I understand this has been a bit of a shock, Angelina. It will take time for you to fully understand how this will affect your life. But right now I'm afraid I have urgent business to attend to." Master Jordan stood up behind his desk. "Please return when you're off duty so we can talk again. There are many questions I'm sure you will have and things you need to know." He bowed when Angelina rose from her chair.

"Do you have to do that?"

Uncle Jordan smiled. "Yes, I'm afraid I do. But, only when we're alone for now."

"Melody and Brandon will want to know. They were there when you gave me the journal."

Master Jordan pondered a moment. "No, do not tell them. They will learn soon enough. We can't risk telling anyone."

Annie left with conflicting thoughts. *How can I not tell my best friends? I know I can trust them with anything.* She pondered how her true heritage would affect their future. The reasons for not knowing facts of such great magnitude seemed thin. *I don't feel much like a princess. I don't really know who I am anymore.*

Annie sat among the flowering trees of Tamaroon

while she gazed at the stars beyond the space station dome. A sharp pang stabbed her chest when she thought of her parents. She tried to imagine what it had been like for her mom to be a princess in hiding. *From what or who?* she wondered.

She had often heard the old tale. They had just discovered food that might save Treya, but were lost when they returned to Tamaroon. The repetition of the tale never made it easier.

Tipper sat on her shoulder while E-Chip listened nearby. "I know star charting has improved, but it doesn't help my parents now. Maybe what my mother feared was true and their mission was sabotaged—and someone deleted the star charts from the Starseeker log. It still doesn't change anything." Annie's shoulders sagged.

"So, here I sit, in a baggie old jumpsuit. I'm 'Jumpsuit Annie' the orphaned nobody. But now I'm not a nobody. I'm a somebody—that nobody knows about. I don't see how that's an improvement."

Tipper flapped his wings and chirped cheerfully. From his striped feathered top knot to his wise little black eyes he was different from all the others.

"Maybe I'm just like you, Tipper—unique in many ways. Tomorrow I graduate as a Starseeker officer and I'll be sent off on a mission to deep space." Suddenly it occurred to her—"Tonight the princesses dance with the new heir. If I wasn't in hiding I could dance the royal waltz with Garret." It then struck her:

"Because my mother taught me." Annie felt stunned. "My mother taught me, because she actually thought I would be there."

A holographic figure appeared beside her. "Would you like to dance?" E-Chip projected her old dance instructor.

Annie stood reluctantly at the edge of the green. "I've always liked the royal waltz because it reminds me of Mom. I knew I would never dance at the ball." She fell resigned into a curtsy and mechanically went through the motions of the familiar steps. Annie knew the dance so well; she could dance it in her sleep. *There are no plans for me to go to the ball. To practice the waltz seems pointless. It was all just a silly dream anyway.*

AMARIS broke in. "Report to squad bay for pod study."

Her instructor was zapped into thin air. Tipper fluttered up and called out in alarm.

There would only be the issuing of mission assignments tomorrow, to mark the end of her training. Why AMARIS had scheduled study-time didn't make sense. Maybe others had not yet completed their exams.

Annie whistled and Tipper flew into her tool pack. He usually spent her study-time in her room and today was no different.

Melody would be waiting and she was sure to go *hyper-static* when she heard there was blue blood in her family tree. *Would it matter to Garret if he knew?*

17

HEIR PRINCE

MICROBES GLOWED on the tritum screen as Garret leaned forward to examine them. "I don't understand why this fungus attacks only the Boannie shrubs."

Master Jordan inserted a sample of bark into the analyzer.

"Blight can sometimes devastate one species while having little or no affect on others. But, we must make sure it doesn't spread to the remaining greenhouses."

Rows of green shrubs bearing fruit surrounded them under the immense greenhouse dome of Gosar. Garret took the micro viewer from the infected branch and slipped it into his pocket.

"So, how do we save the crop from being destroyed?"

Master Jordan pulled at his beard while he seemed to regard the young man's depth of concern.

Garret felt the responsibility for the people of

Gosar growing as the hour of his crowning grew near.

"You are right to be concerned Your Highness. Boannie is one of the few crops that can grow in cool greenhouses of the high mountains."

Jordan paused to examine the tree and he seemed to puzzle over ways to get rid of the fungus. "The remedies we have tried have not worked. But I recall that disease resistant relatives from the wild can be used to strengthen a crop. However, the relatives of the Boannie are on Tamaroon.

"Great!" Garret said.

Master Jordan clearly heard the sarcasm when Garret continued.

"And Tamaroon is just a quick hyper jump to where? Oh yeah—nowhere! How could the smartest scientists in the world lose a whole planet? Especially the fabled planet with gardens full of good things to eat." Garret pulled a yellow fruit from one of the healthy trees. His brow was drawn in frustration when he bit into the Boannie. He considered the fruit he held in his hand. "It has an interesting flavor. It's not only incredibly nutritious, but it tastes good." He tossed another fruit to Jordan. "I wonder what other food grows on Tamaroon."

Master Jordan sat on a bench and enjoyed the fruit discovered on the distant world. "The most promising way to fight the Boannie blight is to find Tamaroon."

"Who brought the sample plants from

Tamaroon?" Garret asked as he searched the data stream on a clear tablet.

"They came from the expedition led by Commander Roeshell," Jordan said. "Bryan was a good friend. It was a terrible thing him and his wife disappearing like that in deep space."

"When was that?" Garret folded the tritum tablet and tucked it away in his jacket.

"It was about ten years ago. Their daughter was very young then, but she's practically a young lady now. You've met her. She was working in the Cinders-of-Ellen."

"You mean Jumpsuit Annie?"

"Is that what they call her?"

"She's a quirky girl that keeps to herself. She never wears a uniform and she's always wearing sun shades." A perplexed look crossed Garret's face. "How did she become one of your students?"

"Her father and I were very close."

"And you took her in?"

"Yes, you could say that."

"She's kind of—different."

"Oh, in what way?"

"She sings—when she's on duty." Garret moved uncomfortably about as he tried to explain.

Master Jordan mused. "Singing is not unusual."

"She led that unauthorized shuttle racing and—she's a girl."

"She's a good Starseeker pilot and can speak with

authority."

"Well, there's this thing she does with animals."

"She has a sensitive nature that animals respond to." Garret's frown had deepened with each response from Jordan.

"I think she intentionally tries to avoid me. I've seen her stop dead in her tracks and walk the other way."

"Now that is unusual," Master Jordan admitted. "Usually any girl close to your age does everything she can to get your attention."

"A lot of good it will do them." Garret slumped against the Boannie tree. "None of them are on my father's list. My duty as the royal heir will be to marry from the royal line."

"Ah!" Master Jordan said without surprise. "I see where the problem is now. Annie is not on that list either, is she?"

Garret looked intently at Master Jordan and tried to read how he felt about his interest in Annie. Jordan's undisturbed manner made him decide to tell Master Jordan his true feelings. "Annie isn't a snobbish royal who expects everything done for her. She doesn't hide or twist truth to get what she wants." He sighed before he walked away from the tree. "I can't seem to stop thinking about her. There's something more real about her. She speaks what is on her mind. The worst part is I seem to keep running into her."

Master Jordan seemed flustered at this. "Surely

not, Your Highness! I know you are intelligent enough to see it is only a coincidence."

Garret hung his head in thought. "I don't know about that." His eyes rose full of doubt. "I don't know if I am intelligent enough—I don't know if I am wise enough to rule an entire world." A desperate sarcasm crept into his voice. "I could lead us all into some huge catastrophe that destroys us all?"

Garret looked toward the towers of Gosar palace. He was clearly distracted. "Master Jordan, When the ice returns, the world will die."

"Yes, your majesty, but only if we don't do everything we can to survive." Master Jordan's eyes narrowed with understanding. "I see now what truly brought you here this morning, Your Highness."

Garret faced Jordan "I don't think I can be the king everyone expects me to be."

"Every good king in history has had the same doubts, Garret. You are not alone in this. It's true you'll have many important decisions put on your shoulders. But, you have many qualities that a good leader needs. You're observant and listen well. You know how to analyze and solve problems. You have a sound understanding of many things that will help you make wise decisions. "

"I thought I did," Garret said. "But there is so much I don't know."

Master Jordan seemed aware that the prince was searching for reassurance. "It is a wise man who realizes how much he does not know and when it is time to seek help for answers. You will not be expected to know everything. But, you will be expected to know how to find answers. The more you learn about how things work; the better you will know what is best for Treya. There will be times when you make a decision and will find yourself opposed by others. But, often a time for calm reasoned reflection will clearly prove what is best."

Garret sat down and sighed as he considered this.

I would advise you that your first priority is to support the Starseeker mission to feed the people of Treya. It may mean the survival of our people—of all people. We have not found any others like us beyond this world."

Garret's brow creased.

"Try not to worry too much, Garret. Remember that above all, a good leader is first and foremost a servant. I serve as instructor for the Starseeker Corp and as a Guardian of the royal house, but, many see me as a leader. Just as I serve, you will also serve and lead the people.

"Guardian? How are you a member of the secret royal Guard?"

"You know of the Guard?"

"Like you just said, I'm not stupid. I've heard tales about the secret Guardians since I was a boy. So what do you do in the Guard?"

"Let us just say I am a leader among many and

that you are well protected."

Jordan checked the time. "Our time has grown short I'm afraid. As a Guardian I have much to prepare. Today you're eighteen and become the crown heir. I'm sure the palace has many things for you to do. You can't hide out here all day."

"Thanks," Garret said with a sheepish grin. "Thank you for listening—and I suppose I should now also thank you for guarding me my whole life."

Garret reluctantly let Jordan hustle him off to the palace. Rick and Curt met him at the greenhouse door.

"So did you two know about Master Jordan being a Guardian?

"Yes, Your Highness." Curt gave a short bow. "Information about the Guardians is on a need to know basis."

"Why am I always the last one to know?"

Once the Gosar prince was safely on his way, Master Jordan left the greenhouse in haste.

18

LYRICAL DIVERSION

"WHERE HAVE YOU BEEN?" It was midmorning when Melody greeted Annie at their squad bay door. A guard stood by the stairway nearby and others patrolled entries to the cadet cabin deck.

Melody had a strained expression and was like a static charge ready to burst. Even without a clue she was ready to go suborbital.

"Cool your jets, Mel! You look like you're having a meltdown."

"I can't believe—you have no idea—," Melody sputtered and followed Annie through the squad bay. They punched out some food from the meal minder on their way to her room.

"You're not going to believe it, Mel. I'm finding it hard to believe myself." Melody was all ears when Annie told her what her mother's journal and Master Jordan had said. Their meal was devoured while

Melody hung on every word.

"My mother is the missing princess of Nethas," Annie began.

Melody's mouth hung open and stared in disbelief. "But—How?"

Melody remained speechless while Annie reported all she knew. Afterward, they leaned back on her bed.

"I can't believe Master Jordan and your Aunt never told you."

"Like I said, they were trying to protect me." Annie frowned. "I still don't know what they're protecting me from."

"Does that mean old king Gythos and Inowa Franchini are your grandparents?"

"I guess so."

"Have you ever met them?"

"Not that I remember."

"I can't believe it Annie. You're a real princess." Melody's eyes shone with joy when she gave her friend a hug. "Do you know what this means? You can dance with Garret tonight at the royal ball."

Annie smiled to see Melody so excited. "Somehow I don't see that happening in the next few tarens."

"Why not?"

"Mel, I don't even have a dress to wear to a ball."

"Is that all that's stopping you? I know some stellar places to shop on the data stream and I bet they speed deliver."

"To a space station? Are you serious? Besides I don't have a way to get to Gosar Palace, and I'm sure it's by invitation only."

"I can't believe you're giving up so easily."

"It's not that." Annie sighed. "Uncle Jordan wouldn't have hidden me for all these years if it wasn't dangerous. You know—all the heirs of Nethas are thought to be dead. Someone very likely had them killed."

"Oh Annie, do you really think someone wants to kill you?"

"Why else would Uncle Jordan post guards?"

"So I guess that means no ball."

"Yes Mel, that means there's no way I'm going to a ball."

Melody sighed. "So are you all right? I can stay if you're afraid to be alone."

"No I'm fine, but thanks for asking."

"Is it all right if I go tell Brandon? He's almost as curious as I was."

"Yeah, go ahead! He would be mad if we don't tell him. But, Uncle Jordan said not to tell either of you so it has to stay a secret." Annie went to her study station. "I still have a music assignment from Master Jordan I've been ignoring."

"Great!" Melody said and jumped up. Her hyper-static ball of energy had burst back into life. "I can't wait to see the look on his face."

"Remember Mel, not a word of this to anyone

else."

"You know you can trust us, Annie."

Annie smiled, because she knew she could. She only hoped that no harm would come to them because they shared her secret.

When Melody left to find Brandon, Celia entered the squad bay from her room. A shimmering green gown billowed about her in the cramped room. Her hair and makeup screamed for attention.

"Aren't you two ready?" Celia said. "Oh that's right; neither of your families are connected with the nobles." Celia fingered the fur trim set with crystal that showed her family's connection. "It's a shame you're not going to the Prince's crowning with us. Instead you're all stuck working the night shift." Celia's concern for them was too thin to hide her true delight in leaving them behind.

What did I ever do to her to make her so mean? Annie wondered.

Tris had entered the room behind Celia. Her amber gown had fur trim wrapped with gold braid. She smiled stiffly and lowered her eyes at her friend's harsh words and followed her out the door.

Melody lamented, "You should be going instead of them, Ann."

Annie shrugged. "If I were going, I would be dressed by now. Let me know what Brandon has to say." A shared sadness passed between them before they parted.

"I DON'T BELIEVE YOU!" Brandon said as he looked for some sign from Melody that this was a joke. "Manogeewhiz! Are you serious? His face beamed in radiant surprise. "A princess? Our Annie?"

Melody had gone straight to the Shuttle Bay hangar to tell Brandon the news. Her excitement had kept growing as she reprocessed the news. By the time she got there, she had become a fiery ball of excitement again.

"I know! I can barely believe it myself, but it's true."

"Quiet down you two." Tad said after popping out of the ship they were working on. "Some things are not meant for all ears." The hangar appeared to be deserted.

"Then it really is true? Brandon asked. "And how does my father know this and doesn't tell his son?"

"Yes, it's true." Tad said in a hushed tone and motioned them to do the same.

"How long did you know?" Brandon demanded, "And why didn't anyone tell us?"

"It has been a closely guarded secret until today." Tad frowned as he looked about for others that might hear. "Annie's life would have been in great danger had others known. We couldn't take the chance."

"Danger? What kind of danger?" Melody stepped closer to Brandon.

"You know how all the Nethian heirs have died," Tad explained.

"Nethian?" Brandon interrupted. "How can she be a Nethian royal? They're all dead."

"Yes, Nethian!" Tad continued. "Annie's mother was Dania Franchini. Her accident was staged to put her in hiding on the Starseeker Station. She married her bodyguard and they had Annie."

"Married her bodyguard? How is that possible if she was royalty?" Brandon asked.

"Bryan's distant ancestry was passable, but that's not the point," Tad said. "The point is that Annie could be in a lot of danger." He lowered his voice even more. "Her identity will be publicly revealed tonight at the ball. There's no telling what might happen."

"Do you think there might be an attack?" Brandon asked. "How do you know all this?"

"I'll tell you later. Right now, I have to get ready to chauffer a princess to her first ball."

"How is that possible?" Melody asked incredulously. "I just left her in her room."

"Jordan has someone who's going to work a bit of magic." Tad winked.

"Oh!" Melody moaned. "I wish I was going."

"No you don't," Brandon frowned. "It sounds like dancing tonight might be dangerous."

Tad looked directly at Brandon. "I want you to

stay on standby with that hopped up race shuttle of yours. You never know, it might come in handy tonight."

Garret's face floated in a holovision nearby as Annie hummed a tune.

Tipper was eager to add his own line of notes to her song.

"Oh, so you want to sing. That's good, I could use some help." She continued to hum along with Tipper while she thought about what to write. "Master Jordan's crazy if he thought writing song lyrics would give me a break. This is hard!" Determined not to think about the ball, she rocked back in her floating chair to think.

"Where do I start?—'Start with what you hope and dream about', he said."

A picture of her parents opened next to Garret's and she thought how one day she dreamed they would be together. But, without star charts a dream is all it was. A sad melody of words began to flow . . . .

Lyric Assignment   ID302Annie2:20:9010
  It's All a Dream —

    It's all a dream, that's all it seems,
    That we'll ever be together.

How could it all be real,
There's no path to lead you home.

My love for you will never cease,
Though space and time keep us apart.

If there's no path to lead you home,
It might as well be all a dream.

Annie's mouth twisted to one side. *That's about the most depressing thing I've ever heard.* She looked at the picture of Garret she had pinned on her holovision and began again. *Maybe if I dream of him there'll be a happier ending.*

New Lyrics — I'll Dream of Him — 2:20:9010

I know you'd find it strange to know,
I often dream of you.
You come and take my hand in yours,
and stars start falling from the sky.

We seem to dance among the clouds,
with blossoms falling through the air.
The music floats upon a breeze,
a graceful waltzing melody.

But dreams are dreams, that's how it seems.
Your world just isn't part of mine.
I know we two can never be,
because I'm hidden from your world.

But I'll come look for you some day,
if you'll just only wait a while.
And I don't care if it's not true,
'cause I'll keep dreaming on of you.

Until then —
I'll dream the dream of him.

That's still not the happy ending I was looking for. Annie posted her assignment and closed the document.

"Why am I so stuck on him?" she said out loud to Tipper. "He's probably a real Nar-bucket and thinks he is the greatest thing in the Meridian Galaxy." She leaned back and frowned. "Celia and her roving pack of aspiring nobility certainly think they are. Why should he be any different?"

Her eyes were drawn back to the flickering image of Garret. There was something different about him, though. His face was warm and friendly and there was intensity in his eyes. She clicked through other photos of him looking through a microscope; holding his little brother; and playing a long necked instrument with strings.

Tonight Garret will be crowned and he'll dance with the princesses. "He doesn't even know I exist." His picture blinked out and she looked at herself in the mirror. "Who can blame him? I look a mess." There was nothing exceptional about her plain face and hair. Her awkward spindly arms and legs had only recently begun to fill out because of daily training. The worst part was the weird color of her eyes. Where they had come from, she had never known.

"I wonder what color eyes my grandparents have?"

She returned to her study pod and began a data stream search for the royal family of Nethas. The royal crest of two seahorses appeared on the screen. It was the same image that was on her mother's journal.

Tabbing through the royal tree she found her mother's family. There was something familiar about the picture of her grandmother. She zoomed in and discovered the same strange colored eyes she had just seen in the mirror.

"Annie!" called a voice over the squad bay intercom. "I have urgent need of your assistance. Can you come out?" The voice sounded familiar.

"Master Jordan? He never comes here." There was no real reason to think it was not her uncle. But, suspicion made her grab her neutron sword. She reasoned that Master Jordan was probably here to walk her to the late shift in the habitat. She picked up her tool pack and whistled. "Tipper, under the lid," she called. Tipper obeyed and Annie turned to the door, sword in hand.

19

HIJACKED

THE GLOWING BLADE LIT Jordan's surprised face. "Good, you're prepared. Now come there's work to do, we have no time to waste, and bring E-Chip," Uncle Jordan said, as he spun about and sped for the door.

Angelina resigned herself to a night of drudgery while everyone else who was a 'somebody' would spend the night in glorious splendor. She could imagine the glittering hall with sumptuous food, beautiful gowns and the glorious music of the orchestra filling the air.

They stepped out to the wide railed walkway that circled the inner chamber of the space station. Each of the ten center decks had walkways with docking platforms for shuttle pods. Angelina was surprised at how many large shuttles were boarding and zipping out the shielded door to the crowning of the prince of

Gosar. She then realized that Uncle Jordan had not taken the trans-tube up to the agriculture domes. He had instead led her down the stairway to ship maintenance on deck nine.

"Master Jordan, what are we working on tonight?" she asked curiously.

"You will see soon enough," he said grinning and stopped before a serviceman's entry. He placed his hand on the ID pad and before she could question him, the door slid open and there stood Brandon's mother, Mirra.

Tears of joy filled Mirra's eyes. "Oh my!" she said. "If only your mother and father could be here now." Her hands pressed and fussed with her work apron while she beckoned them to enter. "Come, come, there is much to do and time is short." Now slow with age, her parent's former maid led them down the hall. "Mind you it's been sometime since I've done this sort of thing. But without a daughter of my own—Oh! This will be so much fun."

Angelina was confused. *"What has Uncle Jordan hijacked me into?"*

Mirra turned into a room and walked over to a storage locker.

"When Tad and I left your parent's quarters we put their belongings in storage until their return." She paused sadly. "Anyway, my dear, there is something here your mother had when she was about your age that I know she would want you to wear tonight."

Mirra passed a key card over the lock. The locker opened to reveal a lavender blue gown that glittered with midrith stones of royalty. The metal flecked stones were teardrop shaped and set in the white fur trim.

"Be-$_{oo}$-^{oo}-ooo!" E-Chip bleeped from the corner.

"A royal gown!" Annie was bewildered. How could this gown have belonged to the mother she had known? "How can it be?" She knew her mother must have had a different life before she was born, but this still seemed unreal.

"Why child, your mother is a direct descendant of the royal line. Of course she would have a gown with the midrith stones of royalty. Has no one told you?"

"She has been told about her heritage, but not that her old nanny stashed away a ball gown."

"Well," Mirra said with a scornful huff. "I see your royal tutor has done you no favors."

Master Jordan stepped forward. "There is no time to dwell on the past. You, young lady, are the only surviving princess of the Nethas kingdom."

Annie considered for a moment. "I knew all that," she said. "It's just that, no one knows who I am, and I thought it was too dangerous."

"All members of the royal family are heavily guarded. Besides you have something to protect you that many don't"

Annie looked at Uncle Jordan skeptically.

"It's on the cord around your neck that you

always keep hidden," Jordan said, "You've been wearing your mother's royal ring since you were six years old."

"Her royal ring? But how can a ring protect me?"

"Give it to me and I'll show you."

Annie pulled the cord over her head and handed it to her uncle. He slipped it from its cord and poked the side with a pointed stylist. The top split in two and slid open.

"Excellent, it seems to be working well." He poked it and it buzzed. "The shield is activated now. Let's test it with your neutron sword. You still have it, don't you?"

"Yes, you told me to keep it with me days ago." Annie pulled it from her pocket and the glowing blade shot out.

"Now, strike me."

"What?" Annie objected.

"It's fine, strike me," Master Jordan repeated.

Annie hesitated, but then swung the glowing sword down in a death blow toward Jordan. When it neared his shoulder the blade disappeared in the light green glow of a damper field.

Annie gasped. "It's like an energy dome, but it's so small."

"Now, set it on full power."

"Master Jordan, are you sure it's safe?" Mirra wrung her hands with worry.

"I'm sure!" Uncle Jordan grinned.

Annie set her sword and drew it slowly toward him. Sparks flew as crackling rays of light were absorbed into the damper field. Uncle Jordan smiled in triumph.

"Only a few ancient rings are still worn by royalty. The secret of their making was reserved for them alone and is now lost. Fear of ring shielded armies was too great." Uncle Jordan took Annie's hand. "You should wear this now where it belongs, on the hand of a princess." He slipped the ring on her finger and bowed. "I must go now to secure Gosar Palace, Your Highness."

"Yes," Mirra said. "If Master Jordan and Tad don't get a move on, you'll be late for the ball." Mirra waved Jordan out of the door. She had work to do.

"Come E-Chip, Annie is in good hands and I have a job for you."

A chill of fear and excitement swelled inside Annie. She was about to dress and go to the royal ball. "I can't believe this is happening. It's always been just a dream."

In no time at all, Mirra had worked her magic. Angelina stood before the mirror in her mother's glittering gown with thin braids of her hair spiraled into sweeps of golden curves. A tiara from the royal house of Franchini was set on her head in a spray of sparkling dust.

"It looks lovely on you," Mirra said.

"Wow, is that really me?" Annie blinked at her

reflection.

Mirra laughed when Tipper fluttered to a perch on her crown. "Wear your mother's cape, dear. The air is very cold outside the palace. So put the hood up when you leave the shuttle."

The soft blue cape edged in gold swept from her shoulders to the floor behind her. The silky smoothness of the dress and cape felt sumptuously beautiful and lifted her confidence.

"Thank you Mirra, so very much, I . . . ."

"There's no need to thank me dear. I'm only doing my duty as an old handmaid to the royal court. Your father's star shuttle is waiting. Tad will be your pilot to the palace. One last thing," Mirra said and handed her a mini datacom. "Use this so Tad can find you when you're ready to leave." Mirra showed her the hidden pocket in the seam of her dress to keep it in. Tipper flew to Angelina's shoulder when she left to find Tad in her father's ship. She walked to the platform in a daze.

I can't believe this is happening! She was only vaguely aware of guards escorting her to the shuttle.

It's all so strange. Standing here about to depart for the ball was an impossible dream only moments ago. She turned in her daze to thank Mirra again, but she had already disappeared. Tad arrived to usher her into the shuttle and they zipped away.

20

IMPOSSIBLE DREAM

THE SUN RAPIDLY DREW NEAR the horizon as Annie gazed out the window of the ship. They descended into the shadowed, white peaks of the mountains and headed toward the glowing palace at the end of the valley.

Annie wasn't wearing a mask but she felt like an imposter. It seemed like make-believe and her claim to royalty was a false charade. But it wasn't. She knew in her heart that her mother Dania was the missing princess rumored to be in hiding after a fake accident. Her father too was distantly related to royalty. Through the efforts of those she trusted most, she now sat in the most beautiful gown she had ever seen, on her way to the royal ball.

"I—must be dreaming." Annie touched the delicate crown on her head to check if it was really there. *It seems impossible, but tonight all things are possible.*

"Only maidens of royal birth dance with the newly crowned prince." Mirra's words from long ago echoed in her head. She was no longer a social outcast and her impossible dream of dancing with Garret would soon come true. A tingle ran up her spin and made her shiver. Her fantasy of marriage to the handsome prince was no longer impossible.

Tad checked the time. "I'm afraid you will miss the crowning," he said. "Commander Jordan has been busy tonight and it couldn't be helped. But, we can watch it." Tad hit a switch and a viewing screen phased into life.

The screen showed the royal throne room of Gosar in full splendor. Banners trimmed in gold draped over balconies and hung in an arch over the family thrones. Garret was already kneeling before his father. The king rose from his throne, took the crown from the steward's pillow and held it above Garret.

"As my father's, fathers have passed on their crown, so I will one day pass it to my son, Garret Olsgood of Gosar." The king then placed a gold circlet sparkling with leaf shaped emeralds on Garret's head, the crown of the Heir Prince.

Annie felt monumental joy as she saw Garret being crowned. The Gosar Prince stood and bowed to his father. He faced the people in the grand hall and bowed to them. A standing ovation followed after Garret hugged his mother and took his new seat to the right of his father. His mother moved to her new position to the left of the king. The right of ruling succession was officially changed.

Guests and keepers of historic records retreated from the central floor to the upper galleries in the side balconies. An orchestra began to play and the royal nobility were reseated at the banquet tables in the side galleries. The camcom feed to the news stream showed the young princesses hugging their families before they departed to wait at the main entry.

Annie felt time slipping away. She needed to hurry.

The King and Queen of Gosar descended the throne platform and began the royal waltz.

"The waltz of the kings!" was announced by the steward. The kings and queens of the other kingdoms were invited to join the Gosar rulers on the dance floor. The traditional colors of each kingdom were brightly displayed in the slow gliding gowns on the floor. The dance ended and the kings and queens of Treya were reseated.

A fanfare of trumpets sounded.

"The waltz of the new-crowned heir of Gosar!" the steward proclaimed as Garret was escorted by bearers of the Gosar banners across the dance floor. The bearers were posted to the side and Garret stood alone before the bottom stair. A young girl of no more than twelve walked to the top grand entry stair. Smiles and a hushed titter of excitement passed through the galleries.

"Maria Kendrick, the princess of Arima," was announced. The orchestra began the royal waltz and the young girl was escorted down the stairs. Garret bowed, took Maria's hand and led her in the sweeping dance around the floor. The watching crowd and a multitude of cameras followed their dance until the orchestra played the final refrain.

"Adel Boscovich, the princess of Caldera," was announced. The dancing couple bowed and curtsied. Little Maria left to select a new partner. A man, who appeared to be her father, was waiting. But, it was Prince Gregory, now ten years old, who royally nodded and took Maria's hand for the next dance. The music played on as Prince Garret walked to the foot of the stair to greet his new partner, Princess Adel.

Annie had been lost in the pageantry, but she now looked beyond the holo screen and saw the castle drawing near. Warm light glowed in the tower windows while globes of light lit the surrounding grounds. She noticed the central dome of the courtyard was oddly twinkling with lights of blue.

Two tones rang out softly overhead and the broadcast of the ball was interrupted. "You are now entering the traffic net!" the pleasant voice of the auto net announced. "Manual controls have been switched to Net control. Please state your destination."

"Gosar palace," Tad said before he let go of the controls.

"Welcome Tad Granger. Please select entry

mode." A list of options appeared in the air.

"Main entry!" Tad answered, before addressing Annie. "Your Highness, the royal waltz has begun. Are you ready to raise a few eyebrows?"

The flutter in Annie's stomach grew in intensity. "I don't know?"

Tad smiled. "Don't worry, Commander Jordan has security under control and Garret is a nice fellow. You've known this dance since you were a little girl. Just take your time and raise that dress of yours when you're on the steps so you don't fall, and you'll be fine." Tad was now grinning from ear to ear. "A lot of people have been looking forward to this moment, Angelina." We're all proud of you and are here to protect you. You enjoy this moment. It's been a long time in coming."

Angelina smiled gratefully at her dear old friend. "Raise the dress, I'll remember," she said.

The ship spiraled around the castle dome and set down at the end of a walkway.

"Put your hood up, your grace," Tad said before he opened the door. "I'll wait for your call."

"Time to go Tipper," Angelina whistled to her friend. Snow blew in through the door as Tipper darted into her hood. She was glad to have the warm cape when she was escorted across the open terrace of the palace.

One of the posted guards stepped forward.

"I am Captain Asher, Your Grace. My men and I

are to escort you to the ball." The captain of the guard offered his arm to her. The tall burly Guardian wore a uniform with the seahorse of Nethas on his shoulder.

She saw the snow swirl about her as if she were in a protective bubble. Angelina realized she felt oddly warm even though the wind blew at her cape. The ring shield did work just like the large energy dome around the castle. The small group then passed through the wall of energy protecting the castle sanctuary, and the swirling snow was left behind.

21

GRAND HALL

The Twelve Kingdoms of
Arima, Caldera, Gosar, and Hincort,
Jantar, Nethas, Omara, and Pollao,
Sethaly, Taspar, Watthem, and Zebron,
All vied for the crown of power.

THE ANCIENT RIGHT OF CROWNING in the grand hall seemed to pass quickly and the celebration had begun. The large crowd made Garret nervous as he acted out the formal bow to the people. He hugged his mother when she rose to give him her seat.

"Remember to smile while you dance with each girl," she whispered. "They'll be watching to see your preference."

Garret forced a large smile that made his mother laugh.

"Do not insult any of them." She grinned. "You

could start a war."

Garret sighed. "I won't embarrass you, Mother." He took his new seat to the right of his father.

Garret's father leaned toward him. "I heard your choice has narrowed to only a few. Choose wisely!"

"I plan to father. But, my choice does not have to be made on this night."

The king and queen then rose for the king's waltz and left Garret to his thoughts.

The startled guard's went for their weapons when feathers burst out of the new arrival's hood.

Captain Asher had just announced to a steward at the door. "Princess Angelina from the house of Franchini," The steward had taken her cape. But, when the hood fell back, Tipper had flown out in a flurry of feathers. They were all greatly surprised by a bird shooting up to perch on a chandelier.

"Stay near, Tipper," she told him.

The guards looked startled and amused.

Tipper fluttered from one high perch to another while he followed Angelina's escort. The palace was an ancient building with high vaulting ceilings supported by an intricate network of pillars and arches. Waltzing music softly echoed through the palace.

Royal guards were posted everywhere in the halls

and entries. Her escort of four guards were alert and in constant communication with security. Crossing the grand entry, Angelina noticed two large glass pillars that had not been there four years ago. They were coral aquariums full of small seahorses. The sound of the orchestra was causing them to glow bright blue in the deserted room.

Garret must have built the aquariums to save them, Angelina thought.

In the final hall leading to the ballroom, the guards stopped by a door. The guards looked confused when they were unexpectedly sent on their way by Captain Asher. He turned a darkly serious look upon her after the guards marched away down the hall. The captain was well armed.

Angelina was seized by sudden panic and she felt her heart throb in her chest.

"My orders were to bring you here, Your Highness." Asher bowed and opened the door to a small room.

If I run he would catch me? Who can I call for help? No one was near. *The mini com in my pocket, I'll call Tad?*

"Please come in, Your Highness, there's not much time." It was a familiar voice.

Relief shot through her when Uncle Jordan appeared in the doorway.

"There are some people here that you need to meet."

Annie stepped into the room and the captain of

the guard followed. It was a simple yet lavish room. An elderly man and woman rose from a coach to greet her. Their faces seemed familiar, though she couldn't place them in her memory.

"Angelina, I would like you to finally meet your grandparents, Gythos and Inowa Franchini, The King and Queen of Nethas." Commander Jordan bowed and Annie curtsied. A pause followed.

Angelina found all eyes on her. "I'm very happy to meet you," was all she could think to say.

"Oh Angelina, I know it's been difficult without your parents," Inowa said. "There are so many times I wanted—" Her words failed and Gythos took her hand. He put an arm around his wife and smiled. "What she means to say, my dear, is that you look beautiful and you remind us very much of our daughter Dania." Inowa smiled in agreement.

Angelina shifted about uncomfortably. "I don't know what I should call you."

Gythos grinned. "We're your grandparents. You may call us whatever you like."

It's true! Annie stood before her grandparents in a royal gown. *I am a princess.*

Her grandfather took her hand and kissed it. "We have long waited for this meeting. The time for your entrance to the ball grows near. There is much you should know, but there is little time. I want you to be watchful," her grandfather warned. "Revealing you as the unknown heir to Nethas may expose you to danger. Relations with the former enemies of the allied kingdoms are tenuous. They question our efforts to survive the ice age and we must guard against a violent rebellion. Our family's distant cousin Kretus Sarvok of Omara now leads the opposition and he is here. But, no attack here would be successful. The castle is too heavily fortified. You have your ring to shield you and an army to guard you. If we weren't sure of your safety we would not have brought you here. So be aware, but know that you may relax and enjoy the ball."

"Gyus, don't frighten her with your politics."

"Nonsense, my dear! When you fear something, learn as much about it as you can. Knowledge conquers fear."

Now I know where the attacks on my mother and her brothers came from. Her grandfathers' words rang true as her fear subsided in knowing an army was guarding against a known enemy. *Cousin Kretus Sarvok must want the Nethas throne.*

Inowa was still irritated with the king's warning. "Come Angelina, will you give your grandmother a hug? I have longed for this day since I last held you as a small child."

Angelina knew then that this was the woman she had seen before. She was the same woman from Gosar palace? It was her grandmother who smiled down on her from a balcony after the new Starseeker cadets were announced. She had also seen her at the royal stables of Caldera. She must have been watching over her all her life. Angelina stepped forward into her grandmother's arms. Tears of sweet regret over lost years bit painfully into the happiness of their reunion.

"I don't know why I'm crying," she croaked, feeling she had to explain her tears. "I'm really very happy."

"I have always loved you my dear and always will. Inowa took Angelina's hand in hers. "Today we will publicly proclaim you as the princess of the oldest kingdom on Treya. In doing this you must willingly accept the responsibility of being an heir to the crown of Nethas. Do you accept this with your own free will?"

Angelina glanced at Uncle Jordan, who kindly smiled. It had never occurred to her that she would be able to reject the crown. To do so would be denying that she had accepted who she was. She looked into her grandmother's blue-violet eyes and said, "I do."

Inowa hugged her granddaughter. "Then you must stand tall so Nethas will be proud of their new found princess."

"Come," Gythos said after he kissed Annie's hand. He led her to the door where Asher stood guard. "There will be much to talk about later, but right now we have a ball to attend. The captain of our royal guard will escort you down the stairs to the dance floor." A warm smile changed the large burly guard into a friendly man.

"Your grandmother and I will stand behind you until after you're announced so all will know your claim to be our granddaughter is true."

Annie placed her hand on Asher's arm and led them all into the hall.

Uncle Jordan seemed distracted as he held his hand to his ear. "Code red, lady hawk has arrived," he said calmly as he winked with reassurance in her direction.

In the hall, two wide-eyed servants looking in Annie's direction quickly bowed and left. Commander Jordan spoke briefly with the king, bowed and was quickly off in the same direction as the servants.

The royal waltz resounded through the hall. A flutter of wings let Annie know that Tipper was still near. The name of a princess rang out from the large room ahead. Asher led her down the hall to stand behind the two remaining young woman. They both wore beautiful gowns. One was fanning herself with a confident air. The last girl nervously fidgeted about.

"Patrice Bonnard, Princess of Watthem!" The steward proclaimed.

Patrice put away her fan and took the arm of her escort. Without seeming to notice anyone else, she proudly walked through the ballroom entry and down the stairway. The guests in the galleries continued to murmur. Gossip about the girls continued in a steady stream on the monitor by the door. The dance floor had filled with the girls who had chosen new partners after their dance with the prince.

"Sandra Thedwick, Princess of Zebron!"

Sandra had been nervously glancing at Angelina's party. She looked distressed when she took her escort's arm and stepped awkwardly toward the stairs. Titters of amusement could be heard within the wave of gossip that followed her entry.

Asher walked Angelina to the doorway. The crowd began to whisper and point in her direction. The midrith stones on Angelina's gown proclaimed her royal heritage. But her grandparents behind her proclaimed her as an heir to a royal line thought to be dead. The murmur of gossip soon died and the faces of the crowd turned to the unknown girl on the stair. The galleries grew quiet.

A shiver ran up Angelina's spin. *What am I doing here?* she thought. *Maybe it's not too late to turn and run.*

CLANG! The sound of metal against marble rang out and broke the peaceful night. A bronze knight riding a winged horse toppled to the floor in a distant hall of the palace. Uniformed guards struggled to contain armed invaders as a force of intruders in black slipped by. Arriving reinforcements pursued the attackers who fled into the shadows.

Captain Trent smacked the podcom on his wrist.

"Outer ring breached by black knights at east gate – breach at east gate."

"Code red," came the responding command. "Lady hawk has arrived."

"Reinforce inner containment shield," the Captain spat with a new surge of urgency. "Grey owl is presenting lady hawk. Code red – repeat CODE RED!" The armaments of his men rattled behind him as he ran.

22

ROYAL WALTZ

THE CROWD WAS SILENT when Angelina reached the top of the stairs. Her throbbing heart pounded in her chest and rang in her ears. She swallowed hard and looked into the questioning faces of hundreds of nobles. They had come for the crowning of the new Gosar heir and were now presented with a new-found heir to the ancient kingdom of Nethas. The Royal Waltz ended and the music echoing among the marble pillars. A murmur rose like an ocean wave at her unexpected arrival and then fell away into silence. Her legs trembled, but she forced herself to stand tall and poised for her grandparents behind her and the people of Nethas that she had never met.

"Angelina Franchini, Princess of Nethas!"

A shockwave of surprise rebounded through the crowd and fell away. The click of Garret's boots rang through the hushed Grand Hall as he came to receive her.

Annie felt frozen at the top of the stairs. *Will he recognize me?* she wondered. *Will he think I deceived him because I never told him who I am?*

Asher extended his arm and guided her slowly down the stairs. Angelina's blue-violet eyes were locked with Garret's until she arrived at the bottom of the stairs.

"Princess Angelina?" Garret asked before he took her hand.

"Yes, Your Highness," she murmured. He drew her up from her timid curtsy and his strong hands swept her gracefully out onto the floor. His confident smile eased her fears and she no longer heard the whispering crowd.

Garret nodded to the conductor, who quickly restarted the Royal Waltz. The Prince smiled and took her in his arms across the dance floor.

Angelina glided along in the familiar dance as the room and people around them became a blur. The music resounded sweetly through the hall with more depth than she had ever heard before.

Garret looked down at her. "You're the last person I expected to see at the end of this line." A questioning look creased his brow. "I don't remember your eyes being that color before," he said.

Angelina felt her confidence crumble and she blushed before lowering her eyes.

Garret suddenly looked unsure of himself. "I'm

sorry," he said, and stumbled off balance. "I didn't mean to embarrass you."

His sudden concern made her laugh. "So the prince is human after all." Her smile widened when she looked up into his dark brown eyes.

The corner of his mouth curled up and his gaze lingered on her face. "How are you're here—the princess of Nethas?"

"I don't know," Annie confessed. "It all seems impossible." She giggled in disbelief.

All else around her melted away while the enchanting music played on.

The Royal Waltz again came to an end and the orchestra began a new dance. Other couples came to the floor. Questioning looks from nobility flashed around them. Curious reporters pushed towards them and were ready to pounce.

Annie saw them approaching and a panic grew inside her as she worried about what she could possibly say.

Garret also seemed aware and looked around the grand hall. "I think now is the time for a discreet exit."

Angelina found herself dancing past the throne platform and through a guarded doorway.

Garret had led her to an empty hall with guards posted at the far end. Annie was surprised to find she was alone with the prince for the first time.

"Sorry," Garret said when he saw the surprise on her face. "I felt like a fish in a pond surrounded by hungry cats."

Angelina laughed. His mischievous look reminded her of the time she saw him chasing his brother through the palace.

Ballroom guests entered the far end of the hall and pointed in their direction. Garret led Angelina quickly down a side hall and into a room to escape the following crowd. The familiar flutter of wings passed through the door overhead.

The guards at the doorway looked surprised.

"Don't let anyone in," Garret directed. He then pulled Annie into the cool room and closed the door behind them.

* * * * *

The old royal guard on the throne platform nervously tapped his ear bud communicator. "Hello, can anyone hear me? Pegasus two and Ladyhawk have left containment by the throne. Repeat Pegasus two and Ladyhawk left the inner shield."

The two guardians outside the palace garden smiled at the flustered old guard's report. One responded in a way to calm all those listening that they had everything under control. "Pegasus two and Ladyhawk secured in Tamaroon house." Though there had been a minor skirmish at the outer wall, the post to guard plants, had always been the lightest duty a guard could pull. It was the lowest ranked target zone in the palace and its locking doors to maintain the habitat made it a safe haven. The two guards confidently took up their post.

*   *   *   *   *

Angelina was relieved they had escaped the fishbowl, and was excited that Garret had pulled her into his game of *hide-and-seek*. But, she was nervous to see what he would say or do next.

His gaze made her feel awkward and warmth rushed to her cheeks. The sound of falling water in a fountain caught her attention and Garret followed her retreat across the room.

Stars above the clear ceiling softly lit a central garden of trees, shrubs and flowers. It seemed more beautiful than the splendor of the grand hall.

Garret leaned against the stone rail around the garden, just inches away from her.

"The last time we met you looked like you had seen a scary beast. You're not afraid of me are you?"

"No, Your Highness."

"Please, call me Garret—after all we're alone."

"No, I'm not afraid of you, Garret." She nervously stepped away and he followed her again. "Please call me Annie. I'm not use to the name Angelina." She remembered how frightened she had been, of the shadowy men that day at the track tube. "I had just learned my mother was a princess in hiding, and by being the only heir of Nethas my life is somehow in danger. I didn't know why three men were waiting by the track tube exit."

Garret's head rolled to the side in understanding.

"So, your identity has been kept from you along with everyone else." He paused for a time in thought. "I suppose Master Jordan has always known."

"How did you guess?"

"I believe the old goat is cagier than he leads others to believe."

Annie felt compelled to confide her similar suspicion. "I think he's some sort of secret agent."

Garret's eyebrows rose. "I wouldn't be surprised." Something behind her caught his attention. "Come, let me show you something." He took her hand in his and they strolled to the center of the garden.

Annie didn't know what to expect. He put his arm around her and pointing up in the trees. "They don't turn pink like seahorses but they do remind me of them." Blue fireflies flashed among the leaves in a glowing canopy overhead. The orchestra could be heard faintly down the hall. Time seemed suspended while they watched the blue lights dart about overhead. She laid her head on his shoulder and all else melted away.

A bird chirped nearby and Annie spied her friend in a tree. "Tipper, you found a Boannie tree."

Garret laughed. "I don't know another girl who could identify those."

Annie lifted Tipper from a low branch. "Tipper, I'd like you to meet Prince Garret of Gosar. Garret this is Tipper of Tamaroon."

Tipper suddenly flew up into the trees and gave a

panicked warning call.

"What's wrong?" Garret asked.

"I don't know. I've never seen him like this."

A shadow moved in the balcony above.

"I think it's time for us to leave," Garret said quietly and pulled her towards him. "Just start walking to the door in the corner."

Something dark suddenly zipped past her ear and she jumped in fright.

Blue lasers thrummed up into the balcony behind an escaping figure.

"Run!" Rick ordered as he and Curt burst in, blasting with laser guns.

Curt handed Garret a laser gun. "We're taking you two out the back." Curt retreated with them into the hall to join a large escort of guards. Curt led them all at a run to the back of the palace. Their pounding boots echoed down the hall as Rick followed behind.

Garret ran beside Annie. "It looks like Master Jordan was right to keep you hidden. Don't worry, the Guardians will protect us."

Annie held on to Garret's hand. Her mind spun in confusion and her heart beat at a frantic pace. Her fantasy of the royal ball was now suddenly a bad dream. Garret's friends were leading guards to protect them. "Your friends protect you?"

"They're my bodyguards," Garret admitted. "I have no friends."

Near the end of the hall they stopped. "Form up!"

Curt ordered. The royal guards boxed in the heirs. She saw Uncle Jordan appear from a joining hall with another armed force.

Commander Jordan addressed her, "Your Highness, Archers have invaded the palace."

Annie first looked at Garret, not realizing he was speaking to her. "Archers?" she stuttered.

"Yes, Your Highness," Jordan bowed. "They target royalty with power shields. Neutron swords are useless against shields but metal swords and arrows pass right through them. We believe that only you have been targeted. Those in the ballroom have not been approached or attacked. We must move quickly. Their force is organized and may be large."

"Power shield?" Garret asked.

"Yes, Prince Garret." Master Jordan explained, "You father still wears the shield passed down from his fathers. It will one day pass to you. But, only if we get you to safety."

"The Sweeper indicates a cloaked presence." Curt reported to Jordan. "We can't identify their number or position."

"I can't believe we're so defenseless," she heard Rick say quietly to Garret. His frustration was clear.

"Reliance on the energy dome has made us weak." Garret replied.

Jordan issued his commands. "Lieutenant Curt will create a spearhead to the evacuation zone with Angelina and Garret at the center. Captain Trent will lead the palace guard to clear the way and Sergeant Rick will cover the rear with the Starseeker Guardians."

"Your extraction point," Uncle Jordan told Annie, "is at the far side of the garden."

Panic seized Annie with rapid breath as adrenaline rushed into her veins. A surging need to run filled her.

Commander Jordan called to the guards. "We must move swiftly. Captain Trent, take the lead. Company, Form together!"

Guards quickly wrapped flak jackets around her and Garret. Her cape was thrown around her shoulders and metal shields were thrust in their hands. She pulled her sword from her pocket and Garret pulled out his sword.

"Bee$_{-ee}$-ee^{-oo}"

"E-Chip? Where did you come from?" Annie looked up in surprise.

"I hope you don't mind. I brought him." Uncle Jordan explained. "He's providing mobile surveillance."

Annie looked at E-Chip. "So, now you're a SPY?"

"Woo-oo-$_{oooo}$!" E-Chip's antenna drooped.

Annie sighed at his sorrowful performance. "I'm glad you came to look out for me. Fly high and stay out of firing range."

"Bee-^{op}" E-Chip's air jets fired and he rose above them in full ready mode.

The two forces merged together and quickly

passed through the large rear doors of the palace. The guards raised metal shields around Annie and Garret and they ran from the palace into the dark of night.

23

BROKEN DREAM

THE GOSSIPING CROWD in the ballroom was unaware of the invasion and the orchestra continued to lead the dancing. The revelation of the Nethas heir and the Prince disappearing with her, fed the flames of rumor and speculation.

Celia was caught up in the milling crowd by the circle of fashionable nobles of Omara. She had intentionally dressed in their trendy fashion and had hovered at the outer edge of their circle all night.

"I think Prince Garret has known about her all along," Celia proclaimed loud enough to snag the attention of Omara nobles standing nearby.

Her attempt to join in the conversation with the nobles was again thwarted. Though the group nearby picked up the topic of her speculation, they did not include her in conversation directly.

Tris had loyally stood with Celia all night, but her

attention was drawn elsewhere. She continued glancing at a young guard with a friendly face. He was not unaware of her attention. Once he was caught looking and his face had reddened. This had in turn brought a pink flush to her cheeks. When she glanced back, she saw him leave with other guards down the hall leading to the back of the palace.

"Something's going on," Tris whispered to Celia. "Guards have been sent to the back of the palace. Do you think they know where Prince Garret went?"

"Well of course, Silly," Celia said as she flustered to explain. She lowered her voice so no others would hear. "The Prince always has a large escort. He must have retreated to the royal parlor. Come along," she coaxed Tris. "Ladies of nobility are always welcome there."

They retreated from the crowd to follow the guards.

Kretus Sarvok also saw the guards retreat. He was surveying the crowd from a darkened archway. "Follow the Guardians and find out where this mystery princess came from," he whispered to Ajax, his adviser. "I want this problem resolved before dawn. I will not have our plans changed. If she escapes there will be no other option to war."

Ajax stepped aside to issue the order on his headset. Knights of Omara stationed on the balcony and main floor received the call. Dark uniformed figures quietly left the fringes of the ballroom and disappeared down the back halls.

Annie charged out into the night with her sword raised. The armed regiment flew down the stairway into the dark garden. E-Chip sputtered and bleeped excitedly overhead. Shadows cast by trimmed hedges flickered by. An arrow whizzed overhead and was quickly followed by a hissing cascade of arrows. They hit the guards' shields with the force of hail stones. The storm of so many arrows at one time proved the invaders were many. The attack spurred the escort into a sprint to the central fountain. E-Chip darted about firing blue bursts of light in all directions. Green laser beams cut through the darkness and were absorbed by shields and flack pads on the guards. One guard fell with a hushed cry and disappeared into the shadows behind them.

"He'll be okay," Garret told Annie.

"The ship has arrived on the far side of the garden," Uncle Jordan said. He issued orders into his headset.

A sudden burst of arrows screamed out of the darkness towards Annie. Jordan's hand grabbed her arm but it was too late to pull her out of the way. Shock spread on their faces before the arrows struck.

A pelting thud resounded as the arrows without reason stopped short. Garret had raised his shield just in time to knock them away. A look of surprise was on Jordan's face as he also raised his shield in front of Annie. The metal arrows designed to penetrate the energy shield had deflected away.

"Your reflexes have improved," Master Jordan said with a grin.

Garret smiled in relief and looked over Annie with concern. Their eyes met briefly in a frozen moment.

Tipper's warning call rang out overhead.

A loud roar of voices came from ahead and dark figures tore out of the hedges to block their path. The escort came to a halt. A similar outcry came from behind. Not only were they surrounded, but they were also cut off from their forward and rear guard. The neutron swords of their guards flared into thrumming life about them. There was an immediate clash against the humming beams of the enemy's sparking swords.

"Stay behind me," Garret said before he stepped in front of Annie.

The guards in front of them were being pressed. Garret and Angelina were forced back towards the fountain. Garret hacked aside an attacker who had broken through. It was clear their numbers would soon be overwhelmed. Annie climbed on to the wide rim of the fountain. She whirled about throwing back her cape to defend Garret's back and make a last stand. She steadied herself and held her shield and sword high. *Stop shaking!* she told her arms and willed them to be steady. *You can't be afraid,* she told herself. *Not yet, not now.*

Incredibly, Rick and Curt jumped into the action, forcing their way back to defend the Heir Prince. The powerful cutting force of their blades pushed back enemy fighters as Annie heard a new sound in the garden. A fresh assault to the rear of the enemy was being waged. The forceful tide of the onslaught began to ebb.

Rick, Curt and Garret began their own press with Commander Jordan and slowly gained ground away from the fountain. Angelina remained on the fountain rim holding her shield and sword.

The fountain spray curiously began to sink down slowly. An invisible bubble seemed to press against the plumes of water. It wasn't until she felt the spray bouncing off the bubble that Annie's heart jumped and she took notice. An unseen force was only a few feet away.

"Annie!" a voice called. "Annie, over here!" Annie was stunned with relief when she heard Brandon's voice.

Tipper gave his warning cry, flew past her and glided into a doorway that floated above the fountain rim.

"What are you waiting for?" Brandon asked with a huge toothy smile. "We've gotta fly!"

Annie was never happier to see her floppy haired friend. An arrow hissed by her head as it cut through the air. She dropped her shield to pick up her skirts and ran for the door while arrows hissed all around her. She leaped for the doorway but her hand slipped on the grab bar. She felt herself start to fall away from the ship, but Brandon and Melody helped haul her inside. She looked back and called out to Garret who had turned about to look for her. Her cry was not heard over cheers as their enemy turned to run. The ship was rising when she saw his face one last time before the door closed between them.

"We have to get Garret!" she exclaimed.

"Orders were to just get you," a voice answered from the pilot's helm. Tad was flying the Phantom.

She cried out in protest but knew it was futile and stumbled back from the door. Garret would be safe at his palace home with his guards.

"Are you hurt?" Melody asked as her hands flew in a search over her cape.

"No, I'm fine." She noticed Melody was prodding her left side. Looking down she found an arrow had pierced through her cloak and was still lodged there.

"You think that's bad? Look at this one." Brandon lifted the shaft of another arrow that pierced through the base of her hood.

"Star busters!" Annie shuddered. "I didn't

realize."

"Yea," Brandon said. "How could you not realize you were almost shish-kabob. You would have had the shortest reign in princess history if we hadn't shown up."

Brandon's wiry grin chased away her fears. "I was never happier to see you," she admitted. The new cloaking shield is amazing. I couldn't see or hear the ship when you were only a few feet away."

"I know—I'm awesome." Brandon gloated, but suddenly sobered. "Seriously Annie, you're lucky to be alive right now. What were you thinking standing up on that fountain? Were you trying to be the perfect target?"

"I guess I wasn't thinking." Annie lowered her head as she realized what she had done. "They had backed us up to the fountain and I was defending the high ground."

"Strange how you were the only one defending the high ground."

"Leave her alone, Brandon," Melody scowled. "I'm glad she stayed behind Garret, his friends and the guards. She should have found cover instead of standing out in the open, but at least she didn't try fighting a trained swordsman."

Annie felt a deep blow to her confidence in being able to take care of herself. So maybe she did have a lot to learn before she could take on a real swordsman. She could also be better at making decisions in a crisis.

If she didn't, the next time she might not be so lucky.

"Annie?" Melody asked when she did not respond. "You know we were just worried about you."

"I know, Mel. I was worried too." She remembered she had not been alone. "What about Garret, Uncle Jordan and the rest?"

"They're fine," Tad said. "The attack broke off when we picked you up. The De-Cloaking Scanner shows their forces are in swift retreat. Commander Jordan has ordered the Guardians to report casualties and to resume their posts.

Brandon's face turned angry. "Why isn't he hunting the assassins?"

"He can't," Tad answered. "The Guardians priority is protecting the royal families that have all gathered in the grand hall. We'll send a few scouts to track them and neutralize them if possible."

Brandon still frowned. All these Guardian rules were new to him.

"Guardian?" Annie asked.

Melody heard Annie's question. "Tad told us he was a Guardian when he explained why he needed the Phantom tonight."

Annie's jaw had dropped. "Tad's a Guardian?" she asked Brandon.

"Yeah," Brandon said, "it's even harder for me to believe. My father is a fabled secret Guardian, and I never knew it. Where to now, Dad?"

"We caught them off guard tonight," he

answered. "They still don't know who the princess of Nethas really is. The Starseeker station is the safest place for Annie. It has the highest security and they can't track us in this ship."

Annie sat back in a daze. Everything had changed so quickly. A few tarens ago she was in her room before a whirlwind of events had changed everything.

Annie looked at Melody and spoke quietly. "So what happens to me now? Do I go on a Starseeker mission or do I get put back in a box for safe keeping?"

"I don't know," Melody answered. "Wherever it is, I'll stay with you."

"You can count me in too," Brandon said.

Annie wasn't so sure that would be possible, but she was glad her friends wanted to stay with her. Her eyes glistened as Gosar shrank away into the distance.

How long will I stay hidden? Will I ever see Garret again?

Garret turned when the dark knights retreated and saw Annie leap up into a doorway. Something shiny followed the shield that she dropped. She called his name and the doorway to nowhere closed. He ran to the fountain when he realized she was gone.

The attackers had broken off and had disappeared into the darkness. Curt went to his side. "She's safe," he said, as if he could read Garret's thoughts. "She'll go into deep cover until we can ferret out who ordered the attack. Her presentation at the ball has brought them out in the open. You, Your Highness, will of course go into lockdown."

Garret frowned at Curt. He then bent over and looked by the fountain. He had seen something fall before she left. He found her shield on the ground next to something shiny. He picked it up and found it was a ring with seahorses. It was the seal of Nethas. Garret sadly looked up into the empty sky. Would he ever see Annie again—the girl with lavender eyes?

24

SEEKING THE LOST
DAY 9

"I WISH I WAS FLYING off to another universe." Annie lamented. *The moment I'm finally with Garret, a war breaks out to kill us both. Fate is determined to keep us apart.*

"Blee-^ee-ep!" E-Chip acknowledged her wistfully while he floated safely in the corner of her room. Uncle Jordan had returned him with several scorch marks. He continued as he had all morning, to bleep responses with sounds that matched her changing moods.

Sleep had not come easy after all that had happened yesterday. The cadets graduated today without ceremony. They simply received assignments as low-grade officers on various ships that would soon depart on missions. Celia and Tris had been surprised early that morning when they had to leave for a nearby star system.

"All the other cadets are preparing to leave on an adventure that could help save our world and I'm confined to my room." She found it more and more difficult to pace about in the small space as her aggravation grew. "Garret, Gillo and the other nobles have probably left as well. It's not fair!" She stopped a hair's breath away from her door.

"BELEEP!" Chip echoed her defiance.

Her rigid stance then melted and she lay against the door. "If I can't go outside this door without being shot, I may never see him again, Chip."

"Who-oo-$_{oo}$," Chip's low wail reflected the hopelessness she felt.

Pushing away from the door that barred her way, she then sat at her study pod. A news picture of Garret opened on her screen. A reporter read the lead story with the title in bold letters behind him; *MYSTERY PRINCESS DISAPPEARS.*

"The mystery princess disappeared with the newly crowned heir of Gosar late last night. No one seems to know why the newfound princess of Nethas has been in hiding. Many speculate about where she has been and where she is now, but no one seems to know anything about Princess Angelina Franchini. This morning at a photo session with Prince Garret, we asked him about who he left the royal ball with, but he refused to comment . . . ."

Annie clicked off the report.

"No one would guess to look up in the clouds, I suppose," she mused.

"Blee-^{eep}-^{eep}," Chip chittered in amusement.

A soft holographic image of Garret's friendly face floated beside the study pod. The lyrics she had written earlier came up on the screen.

She sadly took stock of the short verse. "So much has changed in only a day."

"Bee-$_{yoo}$-ee," E-chip toned.

Annie hummed a line of song and began to enter new text.

New Lyrics II — My Dream Came True — 2:22:9010

Time has rewritten many things
and I'm not who I use to be;
for in the trappings of your world,
I found a new reality.

Though it was impossible it seemed,
I found a way into your world.
And then my dream of you came true,
the day you took me in your arms.

It seemed a dream the day we danced.
You smiled as though you truly cared.
Your eyes reached in and touched my soul
and part of me is with you still.

So now you're always on my mind,
I hope you feel the same way too.
I pray you'll look for me one day,
For your world is part of my world now.

Without you,
I'm just the Flower of Tamaroon.

A tear streaked down her cheek and she blacked the screen out. She sat on her bed and drew up her knees to brood.

My mere existence has spun the whole Treyian world one step closer to the brink of war, she thought helplessly. *I have no control over what happens to me*, she thought. She wished her mom and dad had never left.

I finally met my grandparents, and they turn out to be the King and Queen of Nethas, she thought. *But, here I still am, just Jumpsuit Annie. It seems impossible that I could ever rule a kingdom. Maybe it would be best if I just stay hidden?*

She rolled over on her side and closed her eyes. To say that it had been a stressful day was the understatement of the millennium.

25

JUMPSUIT ANNIE
DAY 10

ANNIE ATTACKED the curving walls of the speed tube the next morning with a vengeance. Security of the space station had been established and Master Jordan allowed her out of her room. Her pent up energy exploded in her morning exercise after being driven half-crazy by confinement. "For the time being, the speed tube is the easiest exercise area to monitor and secure." Uncle Jordan had said.

Her guards had been talking quietly to each other but stopped when Annie entered the warm up chamber. She felt uncomfortable having people waiting on her. They had even hung her jacket and straitened her shoes. Was this what it would be like to live in a palace? Her things would never again stay where she tossed them and someone would always be watching.

It was a relief when she returned to her quarters and the guards remained outside her door. She felt like making a face at them through the door, but of course that would have been childish. She hated to be called childish, especially when everyone she knew was older than her.

Why was their presence so irritating? Perhaps it was because they reminded her of danger from the unknown enemy who wanted her dead. It was a danger she neither earned nor deserved and she wanted to kick, claw and spit into the eye of whoever it was that threatened her. *A lot of good that would do,* she thought. Her near escape in the palace garden proved she wasn't ready to meet her enemy. *I'd end up like shish-kabob, as Brandon said.*

After a quick shower, she brushed her hair and reached for the cord that was no longer around her neck. Her hand was also bare. She missed the remembrance from her mother and security of the power shield. *How could I have lost my mother's ring after all these years?*

She opened the Tamaroon search file on her study pod. News of the day streamed across the top of the screen. The *MYSTERY PRINCESS* was still in the news, but the rising friction among the kingdoms had returned to the headlines.

Annie knew she wasn't the cause of the brewing war over shrinking food reserves and heat resources, but it angered her to be used like a pawn in a grand

and dangerous game for power. At least one kingdom had plotted to take over her grandparent's kingdom of Nethas. There was nothing she could do, yet her life was still in peril. She closed the news stream and returned to the search for her parents.

Words from her mother's journal echo in her mind, "Keep E-Chip close, he holds the key." Why her mother's message was damaged she didn't know. She blamed it on the robot laser battle with Gen-E right before E-Chip recorded it. She played again the garbled message from her mother's journal.

```
"One last thing— ther e's a ... #/~/ /#
... om E-Chip stored in th ... #/*/ /#
... or constructing star charts th at
will locate Tamaroon. Only you can
access this recording and I can't
think of a safer place to leave
it."
```

No matter how many times she played it no one could fill in the missing words. *What was stored where,* she wondered? Whatever it was, it held the star charts to Tamaroon and E-Chip held the key. This cryptic message she received three days ago, was the best clue in twelve years to finding her parents and Tamaroon.

She had already had E-Chip run a full diagnostic of all his files, but found nothing. Frustrated, she picked up her mother's journal and fiddled with it while she thought. She had examined all of the files on the comcord but there had only been text files. None were like those used for star charts. The charts were in something only she could access. The only secured files that she alone could access were on the comcord, and there were no star charts there.

She poked and prodded its sides and flipped the journal about. A speaker popped up; the data stick ejected and snapped back in; the power bar clicked in and out of place. Button controls lined up along its side, but no secret compartment revealed itself.

"I don't know what I'm looking for, E-Chip. I don't suppose you have a clue, do you?"

E-Chip simply bleeped.

Annie examined the scorch marks. "I suppose I should check you for damage." She picked up a pin driver and started checking panels in the blackened areas. She removed them and cleaned them while she worked.

"Looks like you took a hard shot by your memory banks," she said, popping off another panel. "Who programmed you for battle tactics anyway? Was it Uncle Jordan? You would be of no use to me as a bucket of bolts." Among the data sticks she found one missing. There was a loose connection to a hard drive beside it, so she plugged it in. "Strange, you didn't seem to malfunction with a loose wire and a hole in your head." Popping the panel back in place she noticed E-Chip quietly clicking with tiny lights flashing. It was like he was downloading information from the data stream.

"A-A-aa" E-Chip toned as lights flashed on. "A-A-Annie, E-Chip is back!"

"You can talk?" Annie fell back on her bunk in surprise. "Back? Back from where?"

"E-Chips voice animation is back on line. Yup, yup, Yippee!"

"Back you say! When did you lose your voice?

"E-Chip lost voice when Mrs. Commander removed data stick D-5 to record Annie message."

Annie gasped, *THE missing data stick!—the data stick from E-Chip stored where?—in the comcord? Could it be that simple?* "E-Chip you're a genius."

"Yes," E-Chip agreed. "My classification in human terms is GENIUS."

Annie tore over to the comcord and ejected the data stick. It looked like it could fit. It had to fit. She quickly reopened E-Chip's memory bank and pressed it into the empty memory port. E-Chip again went into download. "Text and pod file found."

"Pod file?" Annie asked. "No star charts?" Annie sank in disappointment. *What would a pod file be doing in a comcord? Comcord and pod files were the only two kinds of files that could be secured.* "That's it!" She jumped up "charts can be embedded in pod files."

"Access the study pod E-Chip."

"Connecting!" A connection rod extended out from E-Chip and locked into Annie's study pod. Annie scanned her hand on the security screen with the seahorses. She opened and flipped through files and found what looked like a star chart file.

"I can't believe it Chip. This could be it!" The stored memory from when she was only six could hold the hidden way to the long lost planet. She held her breath and opened the chart.

A holo projection of stars surrounded her. They changed rapidly as the star-trail opened and then stopped with an image of a blue and green planet rotating in swirling patches of clouds. Annie could hardly believe what she saw as she reached out to the image before her.

"Tamaroon!"

26

MYSTERY PRINCESS

DAY 11

THE NETHAS RING OPENED and unfolded when Garret poked it again with a pointed tool. The center rose, split apart and fanned out miniature processing panels around a glowing core.

"Fascinating! To think that an energy field sent out of such a tiny mechanism can neutralize a laser blast. It's mind boggling." He pressed a button and the ring closed.

"Master Jordan said my father has one of these that I'll inherit someday?"

"Yes, Your Highness," Curt answered. "But that is a very closely guarded secret."

"That is what we're told." Rick added from his station by the door.

Since the night of the ball, Garret had a new appreciation for his Guardian bodyguards. The amazing skill and valor they had shown in fighting their way back to protect him had greatly deepened his respect.

All three of them sat about his royal apartment scanning the data stream on their podcoms. Except for a public appearance to prove he had not disappeared, there was little else to do the last three days. His lockdown status had them all confined to his rooms.

"Have you seen any new sightings of the Mystery Princess?" he asked.

Both Rick and Curt grinned.

"No, Your Highness," Rick responded. "No new gossip about the Nethas princess."

Garret studied the girl on his screen and then zoomed back out of the news shot revealing a castle balcony. "I know that isn't Annie." He frowned in frustration. The balcony of the castle in Nethas was one of many false sightings posted by the media. He leaned back with the ring in his hand. "She should be wearing this ring to protect her."

"The Guardians fear she will be discovered if you take it to her," Curt reminded him. It was the reason they wouldn't tell him where she was. He had a good idea where she might be but he wouldn't know for sure unless he talked to Master Jordan.

Garret was tired of being told what he could not do or where he could not go. He was the Gosar prince after all, and shouldn't have to bow to anyone but his father. He pushed away from his desk in frustration when a thought struck him.

"I'm tired of this," he said. "I'm going to go lay down for a while." He saw Rick and Curt look at each other. It was not unusual for him to want some time alone and they simply shrugged it off as another one of his rebellious teen moments. He left the room and shut the door behind him.

The thought had struck him, that even when he was a child he was never really confined to his room unless he wanted to be.

He hesitated and looked at himself in the mirror. He put his hand on it to be scanned and the wall opened. He was soon in a palace hallway where he ducked into a maintenance room. A secret escape route had been built into his room that he was discouraged from using. He found a maintenance jumpsuit that fit poorly but it would get him where he wanted to go. He easily navigated the back halls and service rooms to the dock hiding the T36 Skyhawk that he flew in the shuttle race. Garret grinned for the first time in days when he pulled the tarp off his means of escape.

Security was not yet on the lookout for his departure. He boarded the ship and his flight to freedom was complete. The Skyhawk shot upward and he locked onto the orbiting Starseeker Station.

It wasn't long before Garret arrived at Master Jordan's office. The Guardian by the door was caught off balance by the maintenance man wearing the royal signet ring of Gosar. He let Garret in and notified Commander Jordan of his arrival.

The room was sparsely furnished and displayed just a few odd keepsakes. Garret tossed the maintenance jumpsuit on a chair in the corner. A new digital luittar propped beside it caught his eye. He picked it up and strummed the touchpad with delight. It was a vast improvement over the antique instrument he had to practice on. He sang a line of the old ballad Annie had hummed by the hot spring of seahorses. Thoughts of her brought back his frustration. He shook it off knowing he had to wait and talk to Master Jordan.

"Why does everyone else get to play an ion powered luittar while I have to play an ancient lute?" He could imagine Master Jordan's response. *A king must be in touch with the past so he can lead his people into the future*. Master Jordan taught all the ancient legends and songs that royalty was expected to know.

A new instrument needs new lyrics, he thought. *There must be something more update worth singing on the data stream*. He sat at Jordan's podcom and logged on to do a search. "Search, please," he said out loud, he paused a moment to think ". . . recent songs," he requested out loud. "No, correction" Garret frowned and begin again. "New lyrics," he directed the search engine and was about to say 'go' when he paused. *Whoa, and nothing historic—Nothing in the past—so how about the future. The future only exists in what we dream. Dreams it is!*

He added "dreams" to the search and hit enter.

Lyrics popped up on Master Jordan's pod station. "This doesn't look bad." His fingers confidently strummed a melody in harmony with his bold venture to find the princess of Nethas. Putting words from the screen to the tune of an ancient ballad, he brought the song to life.

Lyric Assignment   ID302Annie2:20:9010
     It's All a Dream —

     It's all a dream, that's all it seems,
     That we'll ever be together.

     How could it all be real,
     There's no path to lead you home.

     My love for you will never cease,
     Though space and time keep us apart.

     If there's no path to lead you home,
     It might as well be all a dream.

Liking the first set, he continued singing the rest.

New Lyrics — I'll Dream of Him — 2:20:9010

     I know you'd find it strange to know,
     I often dream of you.
     You come and take my hand in yours,
     and stars start falling from the sky. *(He grinned.)*

     We seem to dance among the clouds,
     with blossoms falling through the air.
     The music floats upon a breeze,
     a graceful waltzing melody.

     But dreams are dreams, that's how it seems.
     Your world just isn't part of mine.
     I know we two can never be,
     because I'm hidden from your world.

But I'll come look for you some day,
if you'll just only wait a while.
And I don't care if it's not true,
'cause I'll keep dreaming on of you.

Until then —
I'll dream the dream of *(her.)*

New Lyrics II — 2:22:9010
My Dream Came True

Time has rewritten many things
and I'm not who I use to be;
for in the trappings of your world,
I found a new reality.

Though it was impossible it seemed,
I found a way into your world.
And then my dream of you came true,
the day you took me in your arms.

It seemed a dream the day we danced.
You smiled as though you truly cared.
Your eyes reached in and touched my soul
and part of me is with you still.

So now you're always on my mind,
I hope you feel the same way too.
I pray you'll look for me one day,
For your world is part of my world now.

Without you,
I'm just the Flower of Tamaroon.

The last few words stuck in his throat when he read them. "Annie?"

He quickly scrolled to the top of the screen and found her name. In a stunned pause he realized the song must have been about him. He hoped it was about him. He held his datacom against the screen and saved the file. He didn't know if it was right for him to take it, but he didn't want the window into her thoughts to slip away.

None of the girls on Curt's list were of any interest to him. Annie's face was the only one that kept showing up in his thoughts. Her lyrics made it sound like she truly cared about him even though they had hardly been together. *Are they just her romantic notions about the prince or is it how she truly feels about me?*

He reopened the recording of the royal waltz on his headset and kicked back in Master Jordan's chair, but found he had no patience to wait.

Garret paced about and tried to deduce where Annie might be. He let the waltz play on but pulled the headset from his ear. *The first place we met was in the starship hangar,* he thought. *But, she wasn't there when I arrived. If she is allowed out of her room, what controlled space would they allow her in? The track tube, Yes!—But the morning exercise period is over.*

He paced some more. *What sort of duty would she have? Annie knows the names of Tamaroon plants, but that could just be because her father discovered them.* The memory of their talk in the palace garden came to mind. *She had that little bird for a friend. What was his name?—Tipper!— and he was from the planet Tamaroon.* "The Tamaroon habitat!" *I saw her there when I was with Master Jordan, he must have her stationed there.* The Environment domes were at the top of the station.

The Guardian by the office door tried to stop

him, but Garret ordered him not to. "From what I've learned about the Guardians in the last few days, I outrank Commander Jordan and I order you not to follow me." Garret was pleased with the guard's frustration. "I'll be touring the top of the station until Master Jordan returns."

27

STAR-TRAIL

ANNIE COULD WAIT NO LONGER. She had insisted on seeing Master Jordan as soon as her morning exercise was over.

Yesterday, the Guardians had refused to take her on a hunt for Uncle Jordan. They instead made an appointment to see him the next morning. Confined to her room, she had gone to bed late, after reviewing files her father had left on E-Chip's memory stick.

She hoped Uncle Jordan would make more sense of it all today. The rescue mission to find her parents had waited twelve years. The chance that one more day would make a difference was very small. But, Annie could feel the heat building inside her to fight for the right to join a mission that had already claimed one ship and crew.

Two Guardians trying not to be noticed by others followed Annie and her flying droid on their way to see Master Jordan. E-Chip safely carried the star charts hidden in his memory bank.

Uncle Jordan was almost as excited as Annie when she showed him her discovery.

"You say these were stored on the memory of the journal?" The agony on his face was clear. "To think after all these years that I had this in my possession all along is unbelievable. My dear Annie, you have no idea what all you have recovered."

"We just recovered the possible location of my parents and food for our world to survive," Annie responded with the obvious. "Of course I know what we've found."

"Yes, of course that's what we've found." Master Jordan smiled at her as though she were a small child.

"I'm now a Starseeker officer," she asserted, "and can join the first crew returning to Tamaroon. How soon do you think they'll send a ship?"

"Eager to leave, are you?" Uncle Jordan grinned. "Should the newly found princess of Nethas be sent to where her mother and father have already disappeared?" Sober concern replaced his mirth.

Undaunted, Annie pressed her cause. "There is nothing or no one, who will keep me from going. No one will search harder to find my parents than I will."

"I believe you, Your Highness." His thoughtful gaze at her was calculating. "If you are to go on this mission, we will need the permission of the Starseeker Commander."

Annie let loose of the steam she had built to do battle and smiled in amazement. "I can go?" She leaped up and threw her arms around Uncle Jordan's neck and kissed him on the cheek. "Uncle Jordan, I have dreamed so long about going on this trip. I can't believe it's about to come true."

"Now, now!" Uncle Jordan soothed her as he returned her hug and pried her loose. "There is much to be done before this can happen." He picked up a memory stick. "The first thing is to make lots of copies. I will not have these disappear on me again," he said.

Master Jordan copied the star-charts and handed E-Chips memory stick back to Annie.

"Now, I have some details to work out with Command. I'll look for you in the Cinders-of-Ellen when I'm done." His voice became hushed. "I must warn you not to tell anyone just yet. Not even Melody and Brandon. There are others including the Dark Knights who would like this information. It isn't just being able to trust who you tell but also others they come in contact with."

Annie nodded, but frowned at the thought of not being able to tell her friends.

"Making decisions for the good of all is the responsibility of a leader," he reminded her.

Annie remembered this lesson but never dreamed it would one day apply to her. She had always felt responsible, but it was different thinking how her decisions would affect the good of the people. She truly disliked not being able to share her discovery with Melody and Brandon. She believed Uncle Jordan knew what was best and respected his judgment. She would tell Melody and Brandon in time, but not yet.

The Guardians had swept the Cinders-of-Ellen habitat before finally taking their posts outside the entry. It wasn't like Annie had guards following her everywhere. But, there were Guardians posted everywhere on the station that were watching her at all times.

She made a few routine checks before sitting down on the grassy rise. Tipper hopped down from her shoulder and started pecking about in the grass.

E-Chip hovered about nearby doing his own checks. He managed only to ruffle the fur of the striped Chitter Mice who kicked up sprays of dirt after scolding him.

Annie gazed up at the scattered stars that spread on into the night. "It never ends, Chip. It just goes on and on forever." *Is finding Mom and Dad too much to hope for,* she wondered? *I have to keep believing, especially now.*

"Forever does not calculate," E-Chip responded after a series of flashes and beeps.

"Uncle Jordan may not show up until tarens from now." She lay back in the grass. "If he doesn't hurry up I'll just fall asleep here."

"Let's play a game!" E-Chip buzzed and flashed game icons in the air.

"Oh, not now Chip." She said and closed her eyes.

E-Chip floated around to the other side of her. He projected a holographic figure that kneeled down beside her.

Would you like to dance? E-Chip asked. "There's lots of space here."

"No," she answered without opening her eyes. "I'm tired!"

The pixels on the dance instructor's face flickered and changed. "Will you dance with me Annie?"

Annie's eyes shot open when she recognized the voice. Garret's glowing image looked at her. She jumped to her feet. "Chip, stop it! How did you sound like him?"

Garret's face melted into the sad face of the instructor. "I'm sorry. I didn't mean to frighten you."

"Oh, that was just too weird." Annie looked at the sad face and knew it was a projection of E-Chip. "It's OK, Chip. If I dance with you will you promise not to phase into Garret again?"

"Yes, I promise." A huge grin was projected onto his face and the introduction of the royal waltz began to play.

Annie sighed and raised her hands and began to dance.

They glided over the green meadow as the

waterfall happily splashed into the lower pool.

Tipper twittered and fluttered about as he followed E-Chip and Annie.

The sound of the waltz reminded her of Garret. *Would it ever be safe to see him?*

Garret took the trans-tube to the top of the station. He entered the central hub where several guards were posted. Garret didn't know what to expect.

"Good morning, Your Highness," a Corporal greeted him. "Are you enjoying your visit?"

"Yes thank you, Corporal," Garret replied in surprise and gave the Guardian a slight nod. "Have you heard from Master Jordan?"

"Yes, Your Highness, He said we should expect you and that he will join you shortly."

"Thank you for the message, Corporal. Carry on."

Thanks to Commander Jordan, The Starseeker guards were being polite and not ready to escort him away from the area limited to authorized personnel.

Garret went directly to the Cinders-of-Ellen habitat and was through the door quickly. He paused. From the door he could see the lower pool through the trees. *I can't believe I made it this far*, he thought. This was by far the biggest breakaway he had ever made from his bodyguards. *This is sure to put Curt and Rick in a very bad mood.* He laughed. *What if she isn't even here, he thought? What led me here? Am I crazy? I have no idea what to say to her.*

Some interference was making the music sound funny in his headset. Annoyed at the lack of logic in his plan, Garret turned to leave. A bright colored bird then landed on his shoulder. "Well, hello there," he said with surprise. "You look like Tipper." The bird then pecked at his headset. Garret realized his headset was no longer on. *Why do I hear music?* It was coming from inside the dome.

Something was moving beyond the trees. He pulled a branch away to see a girl in a jumpsuit and solar-shades, dancing with a holo-instructor. "Annie?" he said quietly. He could hardly believe his luck.

Garret hesitated. *I'll just give her the ring and go,* he thought. *There's no need to make a big deal out of it.* Garret walked out onto the green.

Tipper called out and flew to Annie.

Annie froze in a spin and her long golden hair wrapped about her.

"Angelina?" he asked as he drew near.

Annie's tongue seemed to be tied.

"Jumpsuit, Annie?" He came close and stood before her. He gently reached out and removed her sunglasses. Her lavender eyes stared up into his. "I found you," he said.

"You're here," she said in disbelief.

He brushed the hair from her face and bent to kiss her on the cheek. He had found the mystery girl with lavender eyes.

Her surprised face looked up at him. The waltz had continued to play.

Garret smiled and bowed. "May I have this dance?" She smiled, put her hands in his and they spun about on the green. Petals drifted from the trees as Annie's dream came true among the flowers of Tamaroon.

28

TRUE DESTINY

THE BLUR IN ANNIE'S MIND came into focus when Garret confronted Master Jordan.

"There's something I've been wondering ever since I found out that you were tutoring both of us and that Annie's the heir to Nethas."

Master Jordan had discovered his two students dancing on the green and suspected what was on Garret's mind. "I was not unaware of the advantages in uniting the house of Gosar and Nethas."

E-Chip had shut down the dance lesson and raised his optic sensor to observe.

Garret's brow creased before he faced his tutor. "Did you set us up?"

Annie blushed at the subject of her union with Garret, but the thought of there being a plot to trap him appalled her. "Garret, I swear I was not a part of any plot."

"I know. You couldn't have." Garret said, alarmed that he had upset her. "You just learned about your ancestry."

Annie then realized what was being implied. "Uncle Jordan, did you really?"

"Well, it wasn't as if I waved my magic wand." Jordan grinned. "No one can cause two people to fall in love. I only provided a few moments of opportunity."

Annie's eyes met Garret's while she wondered which moments in their lives had been a choreographed plan.

Master Jordan sensed they were questioning their feelings. "A missed moment here or there would not have changed how you feel about each other. Annie, you've been interested in Garret since the first day you saw him. I mean, it was written all over your face."

"No! I can't be in love. We've only just met." Embarrassed, Annie tried to deny her feelings, but Master Jordan seemed so sure. "Am I really? Is it so obvious?"

Jordan continued, "Garret was just as taken with you from the first day you met."

Garret's amused smirk turned sheepish as his expression admitted the truth to Annie.

"The signals young people send are so transparent."

"I didn't even know I was sending signals," Annie said.

"Ha! That's what makes it so fun to watch." Master Jordan laughed, and seemed very pleased with himself. "The first time Annie met you in class she blushed redder than a rose."

"You mean the first time we met in the launch bay," Annie corrected.

Undaunted Master Jordan continued, "And Garret, you've been distracted since the first day you saw her in the Cinders-of-Ellen."

"Well, besides the launch bay, there was sword class."

"Oh! —well—it seems I didn't do as much as I thought." Master Jordan's smile was just a bit too sly. No one could deny the love struck-gaze the royal heirs now shared.

Master Jordan cleared his throat. "There is the matter of a mission to Tamaroon that brought me here." He immediately had their attention. "Starseeker Command was preparing to deploy a starship to be a refuge for Annie. The Guardians hoped to keep her safe there until after the forces of the black knights are drawn out and contained. With the discovery of the missing star charts, I have persuaded Command to direct the ship on a mission to Tamaroon."

Garret looked surprised. "Discovery of star charts?"

"Yes," Master Jordan explained. "Annie discovered them in her mother's journal that she just received." The regret of lost years tinged his words.

"Garret, I suppose you would want the command of this mission."

"You know that I would insist upon it." Garret took Annie's hand in his. His determined brow left no doubt that he was going on this mission.

Master Jordan's sad concern marked the depth of possible danger. "Very well, Your Highness. There are preparations we must all make. Annie, you'll need to tell Melody and Brandon they will be leaving with you at 06:00 tarens tomorrow morning. Keep E-Chip with you and don't message or tell anyone else. Is that clear?"

"Yes, Master Jordan."

"Oh, I forgot," Jordan said with a smile, "Rick and Curt are waiting outside. You have some explaining to do. See that they are ready tomorrow as well."

Master Jordan left and Garret looked at Annie. "I hope you have my back on this one. Bodyguards really hate it when you sneak away out of their cover zone."

Annie grinned. He was truly a part of her world now.

"Can you believe it, Garret? Tomorrow we'll be on our way to Tamaroon."

29

NIGHT FLIGHT

"Don't you like us?" Curt asked. "You know, sneaking off can get us re-assigned. We've already been told to report to your father tomorrow about this." The echo of Curt's voice resounded in Annie's ears beneath the central dome of the habitat hub.

"I am sorry," Garret replied. "I really didn't think about how it might affect you. I promise to talk to my father about this and take full responsibility."

Rick seemed to notice that Garret was still holding her hand and was all smiles. "I see you two got together," he said with a bit of sarcasm. "I suppose we'll be pulling double duty from now on."

Annie blushed before the smiling young men. It seemed that Garret's bodyguards were well aware of how he felt about her. She wondered what Garret had told them.

"About tomorrow," Garret said. "You won't have

time to see my father. We're all leaving at 06:00 on a mission to Tamaroon and I'm the commander."

Curt and Rick both glanced at each other.

"You're not kidding, are you?" Curt didn't only look surprised, he appeared to be going into shock. "This changes everything," he murmured as he seemed to be making mental notes and plans.

Rick seemed more curious than surprised. "I see the security flight has a new destination. But, how do we travel to a planet without charts?"

"The charts have been recovered, but no one is to know," Garret ordered. "We all need to prepare to leave," he said and led them towards the trans-tube.

Annie couldn't help but grin. Not only was she leaving on the space voyage she had always dreamed about, but Garret would also be with her. She then remembered there were others that needed to prepare for launch. "Garret, I assume Uncle Jordan has already picked the rest of the crew, but we need to tell Melody and Brandon."

Leaving the habitat hub, they boarded the trans-tube. Curt busily flipped through holographic files. He suddenly stopped and read with wide eyes. "Oh no!"

Rick was suddenly alert and reading the file. "What is it?"

Garret demanded, "What's happened?"

"Nethas is being attacked," Curt reported.

The doors opened to the main deck where crew members had started to dash about. Yellow lights warned those on duty to be on watch for attack. The station had gone into lockdown.

Reports of an *Attack on Nethas* streamed across news and information boards.

Rick and Curt were on their communicators looking for information.

Garret turned to Annie and raised her hand. The ring of Nethas was in his hand.

"This belongs to you," he said and put the ring on her finger. "The shield will keep you safe."

"Are you leaving?" Annie asked. Her only fear was that he might now leave her.

"I don't plan to," he replied with a smile.

"The city's shield is being bombarded and a force is attempting to cross the Endoyen Plains to storm the castle," Curt informed the prince. "We've been ordered to secure you and the princess. I suggest we use Annie's quarters."

There was no discussion and they quickly made their way to the cadet lodging deck.

The surprised guard posted outside Annie's squad bay, saluted as the Prince of Gosar and his personal guard entered Annie's quarters.

"Double the guard," Curt ordered when he passed. E-Chip beeped at the guard before following the rest of them in.

Curt continued to search for information.

"Ah, food!" Rick said with delight, and he started pressing buttons on the meal minder. "In times of crisis a warrior must always take stock of his provisions." He passed out food on the table. Annie and Garret sat down on one side.

"Do you think my grandparents are all right?" Annie asked Garret.

"Curt would have said something if they weren't." Garret's look of concern grew deeper. "I'll try to find out where they are," he said and he began to search with his datacom.

Annie opened her datacom, too. "Should I message Melody and Brandon about leaving tomorrow, or has that changed?"

Rick sat down with an armload of food. "No, that won't change." He swallowed so he could speak more clearly. "The Guardians have been planning to pull you two out of here for days. Have them come here so we can tell them to prepare to leave."

Annie put a direct link through to Melody and she began to pick through Ricks provisions on the table.

It wasn't long before Melody and Brandon arrived.

"I had to tear Brandon away from his ship," Melody said. "Brandon was ready to go blast whoever is firing on Nethas."

"What is this?" Brandon asked, looking at the table. "War breaks out and you're eating?"

"It was the warrior's idea," Annie said and nodded to Rick.

"What?" Rick said with a full mouth. "An army

can't march on an empty stomach." He swallowed and looked more serious. "There is nothing we can do about it. Our priority is to secure the safety of two heirs to the strongest kingdoms of Treya."

Melody and Brandon glanced at each other and then sat down to join the food fest. Curt continued to pace and talk softly on his headset.

"Garret's things are already being packed and stowed on the Argo."

"The Argo?" Brandon's eyes lit up. "She's an interstellar ship that can outrun anything." The discovery of an electroplasma reactor had recently made interstellar flight possible for the first time since the original Firestar Ark had colonized their planet. It was a favorite topic of study for Brandon.

"That's precisely why we chose her." Rick replied. "We need to get the rest of you packed and ready. Our time of departure may change."

"The rest of us?" Melody asked. "Did I miss something?"

"Mel," Annie said, "I can hardly believe it. Master Jordan has assigned us to a mission to Tamaroon. We have the star charts."

"The star charts were found?" Melody said in awe. "Is Brandon coming too?"

"Of course I'm coming too," Brandon affirmed. "Are you crazy? There is no way I'm staying behind."

"The charts were with some files on the memory stick in mom's comcord. It originally belonged to E-

Chip. He was able to upload them to my pod station."

E-Chip had been floating quietly in the corner, but rose and came forward at the mention of his name. "E-E-E-Chip is not staying behind."

Everyone flinched back in surprise.

"Oh, and he also had a loose wire in his head. He can talk."

"Yes, I see." Garret said with interest. "That's highly unusual for a program maintenance droid. He shouldn't have been able to fire lasers in battle either."

E-Chip bleeped in annoyance.

"Oh, E-Chip is much more than a maintenance droid," Annie said in his defense.

E-Chip seemed soothed by this.

"His high memory functions are quite advanced. He helped me develop the path selection navigator for the flight simulator.

"Be-rib-it," E-Chip bleeped. "Starseeker Admiral was ple-e-e-ased."

"He has files and information about Tamaroon because he traveled there with my father. We can't leave him behind."

Curt sat at the table. "The attack has turned out to be a minor skirmish. The attackers, who weren't neutralized and captured, have retreated beyond the Endoyen Plains. Commander Jordan told us to stay alert and doubled the night watch until our departure. He told me to ask Princess Angelina to pack everything and get some rest. That goes for Melody and Brandon, too."

"Packing shouldn't take long," Melody said as she stood to leave. "We don't have much that's ours on the station and most everything is already packed in case we shipped out."

"I have a few tools I want to bring," Brandon said.

Curt's eyebrow rose. "You better get moving. The ship will leave when ordered and that could be earlier than planned."

They all got up and Brandon left.

Annie stood in a daze. *None of us knows how much time we truly have.*

30

FOLLOWING THE STARS

"ANNIE!" GARRET CALLED, both Annie and E-Chip returned to the squad bay and the door to her sleep bay closed.

Melody left to finish packing for the mission to Tamaroon and the door to her quarters closed behind her.

"I have to go to the Argo," Garret said. His shoulders hunched over and his mouth drew tight. His hand found hers and he pulled her towards him. "I know I shouldn't be worried with Uncle Jordan in charge of security."

Curt and Rick respectfully stepped towards the squad bay door to give them privacy.

"I'll be fine." Annie smiled. Her shoulders shook with a nervous twinge.

Garret's forehead touched hers. "You better be on that ship when I leave," he said with a grin. "I'm pretty sure I wouldn't like it if something happened to you."

Annie was surprised to feel herself tremble at his closeness. He slowly released her hand and drew away. A look of contentment lingered on his face.

Thunder — FLASH — **BOOM!!!** A thunderous clap resounded and shook the floor and walls. Compressed air threw Annie forward into the squad bay — something slammed her head from behind — stars flashed and everything went black.

Annie tried to open her eyes, but she saw only a brief blur of bright light before they closed. Nearby sounds seemed faint and muffled, as if she was under water. She could hear and feel but couldn't respond.

"Call the guard," she heard someone order. Doors opened and feet shuffled. Emergency lights flashed and a repeating siren rang out in the distant chaos.

"Annie? ANNIEEEE!" she heard Melody cry out in agony. "Oh my god, they killed her!"

Annie felt a hand beside her throat as the ground shifted and began to tilt. "That flying door nearly took off her head. I don't feel a pulse," Curt said quietly.

She felt someone jerk and take a breath beneath her. She knew it must be Garret. The blast had blown them both down.

"No, she can't be dead! Annie, Annie can you hear me?" Garret's urgent voice was so near.

"Blast me to the moon! Where is that guard?" The

frustration in Curt's voice was clear.

"She has to be all right," Garret whispered in agony. "Get a doctor here now!" She felt his arms hug her gently. "Annie, please wake up."

She felt herself rise as Garret sat up and cradled her in his arms. A dizzy throbbing swam through her head as the pounding feet of guards approached. The soft warmth of his lips pressed against the top of her head and the spinning darkness pulled her under.

Public message boards and vid-screens everywhere streamed reports of the battle on the Endoyen Plains of Nethas. One report cut to a reporter on the scene of a tragic explosion on the Starseeker station.

"While the Allied Kingdoms battled against rebel forces south of Nethas, we have learned that a young Starseeker cadet was killed in an unexplained explosion on the officers training cabin deck. We are told that survivors are being released from the site as emergency teams arrive to seal off and contain any damage to ship systems and the hull."

The news feed showed an emergency team in decompression suits clamoring around the squad bay door dragging long hoses and equipment. Mist blasting out of a broken pipe added to the confusion of flashing lights.

An officer directed survivors out to the railed walkway. A tall guard with a body wrapped in a blanket emerged with two cadets carrying duffle bags. Their somber heads hung low as they followed behind to a nearby transport tubes. The news camera cut back to the Vid-screen reporter.

"This has been a sad note to report after the Allies victory on the Endoyen Plains. We've been told that the victim was a young girl who had just completed her training. Her name cannot be released until her family has been notified . . . ."

Kretus Sarvok listened intently to the report in the comfort of his castle chamber in Omara. The fireplace crackled beneath the vid-screen. Two hounds slept at his feet in the flickering light.

"The mystery princess of Nethas has been eliminated without anyone knowing." Ajax stepped forward to the side of the king.

"Yes, but the walls of Nethas remain secure." Kretus grumbled in a low tone.

"I did warn you that it was not the right time to strike."

"Doors to the other kingdoms will close and we will be on our own." A scowl creased the king's brow. "Instead of accepting Omara as a new ruling power, they will turn from us.

Confidence twitched across Ajax's face. "Doors may close, but there are always windows."

The small group lead by Curt, quickly made their

way to the launch bay with a small escort. No one with a camcom showed up, but with spies aboard there was no doubt the rebels were watching.

Melody waited on the ramp of the Argo after the others had boarded. She paced about until Brandon arrived with a floating sled of bulging bags.

Melody rolled her eyes. "I should have known," she moaned. "Where are your clothes?"

"I didn't forget them." Brandon smiled at her concern. "They're in the little bag on top."

Master Jordan arrived with a guard and a sled of crates.

"I see Brandon has packed only the necessities," he chuckled. Brandon snatched the small bag on top before the maintenance bay crew took the sled to the cargo bay.

"Are you coming with us Master Jordan?" Melody asked.

"No," he said quietly, "I must stay here. These bags were prepared days ago for Princess Angelina. Mirra and Annie's grandmother were generously thorough. I have no doubt they also packed things for the rest of you."

They boarded quickly and went to meet with the others in the command bay lounge.

Annie was sitting on an examination table beneath bright lights when a hypo was shot into the base of her neck. A scanner bar, sending out blue light, was waved over the back of her head once more. "It isn't throbbing like it was before but I still feel woozy."

"The swelling has already gone down. It will heal in time." Doctor Conner said. Emma the med-tech put the scanner in her pocket and turned off a large screen display of temperature, heartbeat, and other such measures. "You may return to duty, but no physical activity for a week," the doctor ordered. "Commander Jordan has requested you attend a meeting in our ship's command bay before launch."

"Thank you sir," Annie said and held out her hand in thanks. A phase line passed through Doctor Conner revealing him as a med lab hologram. Annie pulled back her hand in surprise.

Emma smiled and held out her hand. "We're grateful that we could assist you, Your Highness." Annie was glad to feel that at least Emma's hand was real.

"You know who I am?" Annie asked in surprise.

"Commander Jordan thought for your safety that the doctor and I should know." Emma bowed her head as Annie stood to leave. "The ship's commander also knows, Your Highness."

Annie thanked Emma and went to wait for the others in the command bay.

She sat in thought until Curt entered and quickly

surveyed the room. His guiding force and the ever-protective Rick parted and the gentle spirit Annie had come to know as Garret came to sit beside her. His hand curved around hers and he held it firmly in his. There was warmth in his smile though concern creased his brow when he saw the medical wrap around her head.

She smiled back and looked deep into the unblinking wells open wide before her. The timeless moment passed and she again became aware of the throbbing in her head. She then noticed the ship commander bars on his shoulder. "So you're the ship's commander?" she asked playfully.

"Yea, I am" A huge satisfied smile spread across his face.

Annie felt joyfully optimistic about their journey to Tamaroon.

Melody arrived followed by Brandon. She sat beside Annie and gave her a quick hug. "How are you feeling?"

"My head hurts but I'll be okay."

Brandon grinned. "You look pretty good for a dead person. The news is already streaming about the cadet dying in an explosion. Garret's idea for us to all act like you were dead was a stroke of genius. Uh, I mean your highness. But then Mel screaming for anyone in ear shot that you were dead is what sold it." Melody's sour expression made him stand and put on a show with his arms raised. "What? What did I say?"

He then looked about him. "Can you believe *this*? We—all of us—got assigned to the newest and biggest Starseeker ship ever built." Brandon was beaming in joyful ecstasy.

Melody laughed with Annie. "Talk about hypertronic overload!"

The command bay had a wide observation screen on one side and an arc of cushioned seats on the other. An ultra deluxe meal-minder with a re-sequencing replicator for long trips graced the wall at the far end of the bay. It beeped and buzzed as Rick was already pushing its buttons.

"I thought the warrior already filled his stomach," Annie teased.

"I'm only testing it out." Rick grinned as he pulled opened a stram crunch bar.

Their attention turned to Master Jordan when he arrived and they all found a seat. Jordan remained standing as he prepared to address them. His gaze paused happily on Annie and Garret's joined hands.

"Today we survived two attacks," Master Jordan said. "The first proved to the dark knights that an attack on the ruling kingdoms is futile. Our forces easily contained the assault and the majority of their force was paralyzed with stunners and imprisoned. The remnants of their army that retreated will be tracked down and the leaders of their force will soon be found."

Everyone smiled to hear of the easy victory.

Master Jordan continued, "The other attack on the Princess of Nethas is another matter. The dark knights have proved that they can penetrate our most secure stronghold. E-Chip identified a spy at Annie's door. It is only by chance that Annie is still with us today. They are sure to believe they succeeded with your charade today. Thanks to the quick thinking of Prince Garret, they will no longer be searching for her.

"Are you sure they're not still looking for Annie?" Garret asked.

"Only time will tell," Jordan continued, "but be warned, their spies are among us. Your crew has been carefully screened and I'm certain your ship is free of them. We are now tracking them down and believe we'll soon root them out. I will remain in contact with you and advise you when we have completed our task. So relax and enjoy your journey."

"All right!" Garret exclaimed with enthusiasm that was totally out of character for him. He dramatically raised his arms. "All is quiet in the realm," he proclaimed, "and we are free to explore the universe." Everyone laughed as the tension from the day's events was replaced by nervous anticipation of what their journey ahead might hold.

Annie felt the same spark of excitement she saw in Garret's expression. *It's no longer just a dream,* she thought. *I'm on my way to Tamaroon.*

A joyful flicker in her heart sprang to life and tingled up her spine as new lyrics from her soul gently floated through her mind.

We'll travel to the stars,
to find the love that once was lost.
The stars themselves will show the way,
we'll find a way to bring them home.

Yes, there's a brand new world ahead,
and now at last I'm on my way!

Tamaroon!

GLOSSARY

12 KINGDOMS - Gosar, Nethas, Caldera, Omara, Taspar, Sethaly, Arima, Pollao, Jantar, Zebron , Hincort, Watthem.

AMARIS – Assignment Manager Assistant for the Rotating Itinerary System on the Starseeker space station. She rotates the crew in and out of the training gyms and dining halls so that they are never over crowded. She also functions as a DataStream communication device.

BOANNIE TREE, Boannie Flower, Boanna Fruit - discovered by Bryan Roeshell on Tamaroon.

COMMUNICATOR - COMCORD - Dania's outdated journal. DATACOM- similar to a cell phone on a wrist band or in a pocket. PODCOM or STUDY POD - station for study or research.

CURVED LASER - Methods to curve laser light beams are being studied with some success.

DATA STREAM - the data stream is an internet of information storage that can be freely accessed by invisible light beams and orbiting message relay beacons deployed in space.

DERIUS MOON - of Treya is ringed by an asteroid belt where the shuttle race takes place.

FLAMWARE - a term coined by Brandon to refer to bright

garish clothing worn by off-duty cadets before graduation.

GUARDIANS - are a superior force of defense that exists within the Royal Guard of the seven oldest kingdoms. They are highly trained in defense, knowledge and the truth of old legends. King Olsgood of Gosar is the leader of the Guardians. Nethas was the original kingdom but over time, the central power shifted as Gosar became a powerful city of trade. The kingdoms splintered as they grew, but the guardians of the old ways & knowledge remained to protect the royal descendants in the seven older kingdoms. Other kingdoms have royal guards but no guardians.

GUARDIAN HELMET - Worn on guard duty and in battle.

HEADCOM - hands free voice communicator. CAMCOM - a camera integrated in a datacom. HOLOCOM - projects holographic visits of royals and Guardians used for conference meetings.

HOLOVISON - holo-viewer that projects 3-D images in the air.

HYPER JUMP - is a fictitious method of traveling faster than light in which space is folded to achieve instantaneous transfer (or translation). Travelers experience momentary "insideoutness." Hyperspace is a condition rather than a location where all velocity is zero and speed is infinite. Navigation requires complex calculations. Jumping near a gravitational mass (or well) is likely to cause an uncertain exit point.

ICE AGE - prolonged freezing weather with glacial ice that may be caused by a planet's orbit growing farther from the sun for a period of time or a cooling cycle of the sun with sun spots.

KASALDUNE - is a legendary land of peace.

KRP - Kitchen Routing Patrol duty performed by lower ranking members of the crew.

LASER GUN - its blue colored beams can be set to stun and paralyze or blast.

LUITTAR - A lute shaped guitar. New digital versions are easy to play with more options but lack a fullness in the quality of sound.

MEAL MINDER - or food dispenser of frozen sorba, zorker burgers, stram granola bars, etc.

MIDRITH STONES of royalty - rare gray metal flecked stones only worn by royalty.

MERIDIAN GLAXY - is the home of the Nubian sun and planet Treya.

NETHAS RING - is a ring of power worn by royalty and projects a protective field around the bearer. It bears the royal seal of the kingdom.

NEUTRON SWORD - disappears in faint green glow in the damper field of a ring shield

NUBIAN SUN - is the sun in Treya's planetary system.

QUADMAR - unit of monetary exchange

RE-SEQUENCING REPLICATOR - is a new synthesizer for food on long space flights.

SHUTTLE PODS - are air transport ships able to leave and reenter the planet atmosphere to and from outer space. They are not equipped for long voyages in deep space.

SLEEP BAY - Bunk room off a squad bay for 1-2 crew members on long term assignment.

STARSEEKER - a member of the Starseeker Corps trained to serve in research and on space missions seeking new sources of food and possible new human habitats on other planets.

STRAM - is a grain grown like corn and is made into bread-like cakes and granola bars.

T35 Phantom Firestar - is a race shuttle used by Annie, Brandon and Melody. It was named after the legendary Firestar that brought the first colonists. It's core powered the weather station that held back the snow storms. The technology to recreate a Firestar core is lost and its creator has gained mythical status.

T36 SKYHAWK - a fast new race shuttle with a mystery crew

TAMAROON – mysterious missing planet, discovered by Annie's father. He, his wife, crew and the location of the planet are now missing.

TIME: micropec = 1 sec. / minipec = 10 sec. / tarpec = 2 min. / taren = 1 hour

TRANS-TUBE - is a high-rise vacuum tube elevator also used on the space station.

TREYA and all things Treyian – is Annie's home planet, (originally Traeha transformed over *the ages into "Treya." Treaha read backwards is "a-hearT" or if the "h" is moved to the beginning and read backwards you'll find it is "a earTh" that has been rearranged.)*

TRITUM SCREEN - used for micro analysis of disease and is able to detect various cell types.

TUBING SHOES - sturdy boots with roller bar soles that provide traction when slid sideways.

TUWESIAN GRANITE - is a fabricated building material based on those used to build ancient battlements. It is the hardest known material made and does not decay over time.

VECTRONIC - vectronics are used to help maneuver unmanned robotics and vehicles.

WATER LOCK or shower chamber - used to contain waste and cleaning fluids.

ZEBIDON MIST – (fiction) makes the viewing of floating touch screens & holograms possible.

ACKNOWLEDGMENTS

Curtain Call
My deepest thanks to:
My spiritual father, and biological father also now in heaven, Robert B. Butler, sculptor professor, who gave my imagination wings.
My son Greg Gronas, whose ideas ring throughout every aspect of both plot and character. It is to him I give the credit for the birth of a villain and an evil army. After all, it is not I who want that credit.
My sister Deidre Shelden, a linguist and writer, who was an early reader and my first editor.
My husband, Larry, daughters, Kim Gill, Michelle Vieson, and son David Gronas, for their loving support.
My son-in-law Brandon Gill, who becomes a real character without any encouragement at all.
Deacon Bill Krumm, the first to read through to the final chapter and is a staunch supporter to me, his children and many others in their creative and spiritual work.
Sarah Randall, the first young reader of this new adventure.
Tammy Menninger, a fellow writer for her constant support.
Fellow Deacon Wives and Hobby Lobby employees.

The Ohio Valley Writers Network
Joe D'Amato
Dorothy Binder
Debora Hall Bradley
Jeannie Webster
Kandy Witte

The YA Writer's Page LinkedIn Group
Christine Kellogg
David Ferretti
Robert Arrington
Kat Kirst
Joyce Zeller

and the many other artists and authors I have met on-line for their thoughts and guidance.

DIANE GRONAS

creator of

STARSEEKER

lives near Cincinnati, Ohio
with her husband and family.

To learn more visit Diane Gronas on Pinterest